BRIDGET THORN

HER STOLEN HEART

Complete and Unabridged

LINFORD
Leicester

First published in Great Britain

First Linford Edition
published 2003

British Library CIP Data

Thorn, Bridget
    Her stolen heart.—Large print ed.—
Linford romance library
    1. Love stories
    2. Large type books
    I. Title
    823.9'14 [F]

    ISBN 0–7089–9961–1

Published by
F. A. Thorpe (Publishing)
Anstey, Leicestershire

Set by Words & Graphics Ltd.
Anstey, Leicestershire
Printed and bound in Great Britain by
T. J. International Ltd., Padstow, Cornwall

This book is printed on acid-free paper

HER STOLEN HEART

Linda Slater had recently enjoyed looking at stately homes and their antiques with her new boyfriend, Pete, so she was horrified when she realised Pete was a crook and was planning a robbery at The Old Grange. When Linda refused to help him, his accomplices tied her up and left her in The Grange's attic. Fortunately, the owner's son, Simon, found her and sent for the police. Simon was a total stranger to Linda, but meeting him was to change her life . . .

1

Linda Slater stared at her boyfriend, Pete, in horror. This couldn't be happening. She swallowed hard.

'Why on earth did you think I'd help you?' she demanded when she could control her fury.

Pete shrugged.

'Well, your cousin, Jake,' he began, but Linda broke in, her words falling over each other in her effort to get them out fast enough.

'My cousin is nothing to do with me! I've barely spoken to him since we were kids. And how did you know he was my cousin, anyway? We don't advertise it more than we can help.'

'Your brother told me,' Pete managed to get in when she paused for breath.

'Bill's a fool, always has been. Do you mean he's been seeing Jake? Mum will be furious if he has.'

'He's not a baby, Linda. He can choose his own friends now. So you're going all high and mighty, are you? Miss Goody Two-Shoes, long blonde hair and innocent big brown eyes, butter won't melt in your mouth?'

'You can sneer all you like, Pete Jackson, but I'm having nothing to do with your escapade.'

'Right, then. We're finished. But if you breathe a word to anyone it'll be worse for you, and for Bill. Remember that, Linda, my love.'

He swung round and stalked away, and Linda stared after him. What should she do? She'd only known him for a few weeks, and until now she'd enjoyed his company. He'd been attentive, and she'd never before seen him lose his cool. He liked the same sorts of things she did, looking at gardens and stately homes and the antiques they contained.

Every weekend they'd been somewhere new, and he seemed to know a lot about the various places, the owners, and especially the pictures. He'd impressed her with his knowledge of which were original paintings, and which copies.

She'd been surprised when he suggested coming back to The Old Grange for a second week running. It wasn't a big or important house, and he'd said the paintings were all second-rate. But she found him attractive. She herself had enjoyed looking at the rooms, less formal and imposing than in some places, and she was happy to be with him. Until, that was, he'd made such an astonishing suggestion. She fumed anew. How could he ever believe she would agree? Just because her cousin, Jake, was a crook didn't mean she was, too.

Pete's handsome face had been twisted with anger during their heated argument. His dark eyes had blazed, and she'd suddenly noticed how close together they were, and how thin and mean his lips had become when he'd been arguing. He wasn't so handsome after all, when he wasn't smiling, anxious to please.

Linda shivered. Despite the hot sun she felt cold. She stared after Pete as he stalked across the field that sloped gently up towards the house. He paused and two other men, both large, beefy-looking, tough specimens, spoke to him, then they went off in one direction and Pete strode on towards the side of the house that overlooked the formal gardens. She took a hurried step after him, then halted. He meant what he'd said. She had no doubt about that. If she told anyone, he'd take revenge, and not just on her. She didn't mind for herself, but how far was Bill involved? Would Pete cause trouble for him?

She had to contact Bill. She cursed herself for not bringing her mobile phone, but she'd seen a telephone kiosk near where the lane leading to the Grange had divided from the main road through the village. If only she could catch Bill, speak to him, warn him.

Spinning round Linda took a couple of steps towards the main gateway and collided with something large and hard and solid.

'Steady! What's the rush?' a deep voice asked, and her arms were grasped by strong, gloved hands.

'Oh, I'm sorry,' she gasped, hearing an odd, metallic clanging close to her head.

Fleetingly, Linda wondered why anyone should be wearing gloves on such a hot day, and then she became aware of vividly-coloured clothes, emerald green and scarlet stripes, only inches from her face, and stranger still, bright metal gleaming between gaps. She raised her head, and blinked. Was she dreaming? The man was wearing a helmet, a mediaeval headpiece which obscured all except his eyes. How could she be facing a knight in armour? Linda struggled free of the clasp on her arm.

'I'm sorry,' she gasped.

She felt an idiot. She'd forgotten for the moment that this weekend there was some special event at the Grange, a re-enactment, Pete had said, of some ancient battles, and living history displays where people lived in tents and pretended to be mediaeval or Tudor peasants and soldiers, demonstrating old crafts. This must be one of the performers, dressed in costume, though she now remembered that the main historical event didn't start until the afternoon.

'I need a telephone, and I saw one in the village,' she explained, and tried to move past him.

He was very tall, a head taller than she was, and she was above average. She tried to estimate how much the peaked helmet added to his height. He stepped sideways when she did, his armour clanking, and to her amazement she saw him holding out a mobile phone.

'Use this,' he offered, and Linda, bemused, took it from him.

This was getting odder and odder. She tried to gather her scattered wits. It was quite normal for him to be carrying a mobile! She thought the whole idea of grown men playing at being soldiers was ludicrous, but this would save her ten minutes, and that might be enough to catch Bill, perhaps to stop him doing something stupid, even by his standards.

Thanks,' she muttered, and turned away as she punched in the number.

The ringing tone went on.

Come on, Bill, she thought. You usually stay in bed all Saturday morning. You must be there.

She glanced over her shoulder at the armoured knight. He was close beside her. How could she tell Bill what Pete was planning with him able to hear her every word? But there was no reply, not even the answerphone clicked in. What was Bill doing?

'No reply? Perhaps they're out,' the knight said, and Linda turned to find he'd removed his helmet.

Abstractedly, she noted that he was very good-looking, fair haired, olive-skinned, with eyes that were almost black. He was much better looking than Pete, though there was a superficial resemblance. But she was off fair, handsome men.

She tried again. If Bill were out, unlikely though that seemed, he might have remembered to switch on his mobile.

Again there was no reply, and after a while she switched off and handed back the phone.

'Thanks. Maybe I'll try again later.'

'You look worried. Is there any way I can help?'

Linda shook her head.

'No, but thank you.'

She turned and began to follow in Pete's tracks. Perhaps she could talk to him. He must have been having her on. He couldn't have meant what he'd said.

Then she recalled the anger in his face, and shivered again. She'd be a fool if she tried to kid herself it was all a joke. He'd meant it all right, and now she was deeply worried that Bill was involved, too. If he and Jake had got together again, and it seemed all too likely, Bill could end up in prison. She had to try and stop them.

Pete had threatened her. He'd threatened Bill, but if Bill were involved, too, he'd be in trouble either way. She couldn't let them do it, couldn't stand by and do nothing.

2

A distant church clock chimed. Linda glanced at her watch. It was half-past twelve. She had an hour before the first display started. According to what Pete had said, he intended to make his move during one of the battle scenes, when there would be cannon shots to drown out the noise he would make.

She scrabbled in her shoulder bag for the programme she'd bought, and hastily scanned it. The first battle re-enactment was timed for two o'clock. Her knowledge of weaponry was minimal. She had a vague idea that guns and cannon had been invented some time in the Middle Ages, but she didn't know which of the battles listed would feature them.

Suddenly her stomach rumbled, and she remembered that she'd had no breakfast, and their picnic lunch was in

Pete's car. She could hardly go and demand her share, nor would she have a lift home, but that problem could be dealt with later. Perhaps if she had something to eat she'd be able to think a bit straighter.

There was a map in the programme, and on the far side of the house there were several refreshment stalls, she was thankful to see. Slowly she made her way through the people who were already settling themselves on the slope overlooking the arena marked out with fencing in the field below. Mostly they were family parties with picnic baskets, cool boxes, folding chairs and rugs.

Behind the house Linda joined the first queue she came to, at a burger stall. As she waited to be served she tried to arrange the facts she knew in some sort of order which made sense. What could she do to stop Pete?

Supplied with a burger-filled bap and a bag of chips, she found a shady spot underneath an ancient chestnut tree. Sitting with her back to the trunk she tried to recall their visit here the previous weekend.

'The house was originally just a large farmhouse,' Pete had explained. 'Then it was enlarged by building the big hall, in the centre, and this short wing to join them. Later, in the reign of Elizabeth, it was extended again, so that it had another wing and all now in the shape of a capital E.'

'As a compliment to Elizabeth,' she'd added, pleased to recall that much from history lessons.

'The family lives in the whole house, which isn't actually very big,' Pete had continued.

'Who owns it?' she'd asked.

'Their name's Cottrell. One of them made a fortune in the nineteenth century from coal and iron works, and then went into steam shipping. They haven't had to sell up like many old families, and they farm and breed horses. I think there's the old couple, he's retired now, and two or three sons who run the farm and the stud.'

'You know a lot,' she'd said, admiringly.

'I like to read up on the owners before I visit a place.'

Linda had been impressed by his preparations, but now she cringed as she thought of the real purpose behind his studies.

They had been able to wander from room to room at their own pace. Instead of following a guide, struggling to hear what was being said, they had been able to ask the volunteer guides stationed in each room whatever questions they liked.

'Do you swap rooms? Ever get tired of being asked the same things over and over again?' she recalled Pete asking.

'No, sir, we have our own patch most of the time. We only swap if there's an emergency,' he'd been told. 'We know all there is to know about our own rooms, I suppose,' the elderly man had replied.

Linda had been too busy to take much notice of the conversation. She'd been admiring the pictures, the porcelain and silver in several large display cabinets, and the lovely furniture.

Pete had been more interested in the pictures, and Linda wished she'd paid more attention. There were lots of portraits, she recalled, but Pete had scoffed at them.

'They're just copies. I bet the originals were sold long ago. The only genuine ones of any value,' he'd added, 'are those miniatures in the big drawing room.'

Linda recalled her surprise that such tiny paintings, some more than a few centimetres in diameter, could be worth more than the huge panoramic battle scenes which practically covered some of the walls. Small paintings, however, would be easy to carry away. Pete could even slip them into his pockets. He might have tried to do that last weekend, but the guides clearly knew their business, and would have spotted any gaps in their treasures at once, in time to give the alarm before a thief could escape.

A thief! She shuddered. How could she have been so taken in? But then, how could she have possibly guessed that Pete, who had a good job as a computer engineer, would have criminal tendencies?

Bringing her thoughts back to the present, Linda decided she didn't know enough history. The first item on the programme was a grand parade of all the participants, then came a display of mediaeval jousting. After that was some archery, and then the Battle of Lewes, in 1264. After this there was a hunting and falconry exhibition, and then another battle and finally an Elizabethan dance in which everyone was invited to join.

The question she needed answered was when guns would be fired. Looking around she saw a small group of performers sitting on the grass, eating what looked like lumps of bread and cheese, and drinking from either horns or rough, pottery mugs. The women wore long gowns of wool and their hair was covered. The men wore short, belted tunics and soft, leather shoes. She walked across to them.

'Hello. You eat authentic period food, do you? What is it?'

'Unleavened bread, baked on a hot stone,' one of the women replied.

'And ale we brewed at the last event a month ago,' a man added. 'Sit ye down, lass. Is it your first time here?'

'Yes, and I'm confused. My history's not very good,' Linda replied. 'Is it going to be noisy? I believe there are cannon and guns.'

'Only at the second battle, later than us. We're the peasants at Lewes. The only noise you'll hear will be the trumpets and so on, though the commentary over the tannoy can be pretty loud,' he added.

Commentary? Tannoy? Would that be loud enough to mask the noise Pete would make breaking into the house? Probably. Linda looked round her. Today the house was not open to the public. Long side towards them, it

16

overlooked the slope. Behind, well out of sight from the main arena, were the legs of the letter E, forming two courtyards. The refreshment tents and stalls were beyond these, in what she thought had once been a stable yard. There would be plenty of hiding places in the courtyards, and plenty of windows leading to small rooms, probably kitchens and storerooms, which would not be used today.

Suddenly certain that Pete would wish to have the deed done as early as possible, Linda rose, thanked her new friends, and hurried round the house towards the back. She had to stop them. It didn't matter what they did to her, and Bill, if he had been foolish enough to join them, would have to take his chances. If she could stop them, she told herself firmly, he would not have anything to answer for.

It was difficult to get through, since most of the people were going the other way, eager to find places from where to watch the displays. As she approached the archway which led into the stable yard, and from there to the courtyards, a steward stepped in front of her.

'Stay back, please. There are horses coming through in a moment. Leave space, please.'

Linda, with a few other people, pressed back against the wall. Her eyes widened as she saw several horses, gaily adorned in multi-coloured tournament finery, trotting towards her. The heads of the horses were covered apart from holes for the eyes and ears, and there were skirts draped all round, so that only their tails and the bottom part of their legs were visible.

Men dressed in armour similar to that of the knight she had encountered earlier were riding them, each with striking, brightly-patterned tunics over the armour and shields decorated with the same patterns and colours as their tunics and the horses' gear.

She saw her knight, one of the leading pair, and turned aside. It was unlikely he would recognise her. She wore jeans and a simple white T-shirt, which was almost a uniform for the younger generation here today. Besides, she told herself crossly, it didn't matter if he did.

When the horses had gone, the crowd surged after them, and for a few moments Linda could not push against them. Soon, however, they were gone, and she heard the applause as the horses reached the parade field. The loudspeaker suddenly burst into life, and Linda ran into the first courtyard. It was empty.

Last week, she'd looked out of the windows and admired the intricate pattern of the knot garden which almost filled the space. Full of herbs, their scent wafting towards her now, the bushes were too low to conceal anyone. She ran on, past the massive central block and into the second courtyard, where some of the older buildings had been converted into coach houses. Two horse boxes stood in front of the open doors, and on top of one of them which had been backed up to the wall, a man was doing something to the alarm box.

Beyond, huddled round one of the small windows which led into the domestic quarters, were two more men.

'No! Stop it!' Linda shouted, and then realised her mistake.

She should have gone for help! She backed away, and turned to run, but her foot slipped on some hay which had drifted out of one of the horse boxes, and she fell to her knees. Before she could struggle to her feet they were on her.

Strong, rough fingers bit into her arms, and she was hauled to her feet and dragged across the yard. Pete, scrambling down from the roof of the horse box, stalked across and stood glaring at her.

Linda wondered how she could ever have thought him handsome, or been attracted to him. His eyes were like slits, his nose pinched, and his mouth was twisted in a cruel smile.

'You should have done as I said, and

acted as lookout,' he snarled, putting his hands on her shoulders and shaking her unmercifully. 'Have you given us away? Who've you told?'

'No-one!' Linda gasped, her teeth rattling together as he shook her. 'I came to try and stop you! You're crazy! You'll never get away with it, not with all these hundreds of people around.'

She glanced at the other men. They were strangers, big, ugly-looking customers, but she breathed a sigh of relief. Neither Jake nor Bill was involved.

'What'll we do with 'er, Pete?' one of them asked. 'We can't let 'er go, and how would we get 'er to the van?'

'Bring her in with us, but gag her first. I've disabled the alarm. I've an idea how we can use her.'

Linda slumped with frustration as one of the men thrust a piece of rag into her mouth and wound another strip to secure it. It tasted foul, and she almost choked. Pete turned back towards the window. Dimly, she realised that the loudspeaker was no longer just an irritating background noise. Suddenly a blare of trumpets sounded, then a deafening roar of a huge gun being fired. Under cover of that noise, Pete smashed one of the panes.

He reached in, released the catch, and scrambled through. Before she could struggle, Linda was picked up and thrust feet first into what she recognised as one of the small sitting rooms in the oldest section of the house. It had, she remembered the guide telling them, been used by the present owner's mother before her death, and her collection of china, Staffordshire figurines had been left undisturbed.

'Where's the family?' one of Linda's other captors asked as he followed her in.

'Away for the weekend. They're not fans of all the noise and the crowds, and all the staff's helping outside. We've the place to ourselves. We've all the time in the world to pick what we want, and then we can leave this little lady shut up for the rest of the weekend, regretting that she didn't agree to join in with us.'

3

Linda fought then. She managed to scratch the cheek of one man before they grabbed her hands and bound them together behind her back. Kicking out wildly, she landed a blow on Pete's knee, causing him to wince before he slapped her viciously across her face. She fell on to a small, two-seater sofa, her head uncomfortably jammed against one arm. With a snort of satisfaction one of the men grabbed her feet and shoved them together.

'Keep still, or it'll be the worse for you!' he spat out, helping one of the others to secure her ankles.

How could it be worse, Linda wondered as they secured her, but the gag made it impossible to speak, and hampered her breathing. She struggled to draw air into her lungs, trying to twist her head so that the crick in her neck was less painful, glaring at them as they conferred. The room was small, but noise from the loudspeaker came in through the broken window, and made it impossible for her to hear what they were saying. Pete was pointing, then gesticulating, the others nodding in comprehension.

He turned and grinned at her.

'Farewell, my lovely,' he sneered, and gave her a mock bow. 'Have a good weekend, and I hope someone finds you before it's too late.'

He slid cautiously out of the room, and one of the other men heaved Linda on to his shoulders. With her head bumping uncomfortably against his back, she was helpless as he carried her out of the room, along a short passage, and up some twisting stairs. Linda forced herself to concentrate, though she wondered if it would do her any good to know where she was. On their tour last week they hadn't been allowed upstairs in this oldest part of the house.

The present family, they'd been told, lived mainly in the newer wings, and these rooms were given over to storage. Her heart sank. If she was left in a room which was rarely visited, what would happen to her? Unable to move, to shout, draw attention to herself in any way, would she ever be found?

Firmly she pushed away the thought. It wouldn't help. She was going to escape, somehow.

The man carrying her reached the top of the staircase and hesitated slightly, then turned left, towards the back of the house. The passage here was narrow, the ceiling only just high enough for him to walk without brushing his head or Linda's body against the wooden beams.

He opened several doors, and Linda could see trunks, stacked boxes and old furniture. Then, on opening another door, he chuckled and entered the room.

'This should suit you down to the

ground,' he muttered, dropping Linda to the floor.

Winded, she glared helplessly, and then narrowed her eyes. Surrounding her were several suits of armour. In one corner there was a pile of bows stacked against the wall, and quivers full of arrows hung on pegs nearby. Stored incongruously in a Victorian umbrella stand were half a dozen swords, and arranged against another wall, supported by wooden racks, were lances, long spears and what Linda thought were pikes.

The man departed, and a key grated in the lock. Linda's heart sank. Even if she could free herself of her bonds, could she open the door? But at least she would be able to make a noise, and someone might hear her. Although her wrists and ankles were tied she could use her hands and feet to lever herself into a sitting position, and then edge slowly along the floor. She made a circuit, testing everything she could reach, but nothing was sharp enough to cut the bonds round her wrists.

Pausing for a rest, her thoughts returned to Pete. She'd met him through her brother, Bill, when the two men had come into the wine bar where she and some of the girls from the office had been having a drink after work.

'Hey, long time no see, sis,' Bill had greeted her.

He had his own flat, as she did, but he never seemed to visit their parents when she was there. Her mother hadn't complained, but Linda knew she worried. Bill never seemed able to keep a job for long, and some of the friends he had, her disreputable cousin, Jake, for instance, were not the type of men her mother approved of.

Pete Jackson had seemed different. He'd only just arrived in town, for one thing, having been transferred to a new branch of his firm. Bill was a casual acquaintance, met in their local pub a few days before, or so he'd said, but now she began to wonder. Since that day two months ago he'd never mentioned Bill again, and as they'd spent most of their spare time together after work and at weekends, he'd had little time to cultivate Bill's company or meet Jake.

Why had he been so attentive? Surely not just to entice her into helping him by acting as lookout while he continued a robbery? If, as she suspected, he meant to steal the miniatures, he didn't need two other brawny helpers. They'd have slipped easily into his pockets or the knapsack he carried. Was that all he meant to steal?

Linda recalled the horse boxes. If they loaded one of them with bigger items, some of the other pictures he'd dismissed as worthless, for instance, who would suspect? It wasn't like an ordinary lorry or van. There were many horses here today. It could have been the reason Pete had chosen to swoop this weekend, not simply that the family was away and the house closed to visitors.

The thought galvanised her into renewed action, but she moved too swiftly, and fell sideways, banging her shoulder hard on the bare wooden floor. As she wriggled to pull herself upright she heard her shirt tear, and felt a prick in the back of her shoulder.

'A nail,' she muttered, and moved cautiously again.

There it was, quite sharp. Desperate not to lose it, she manoeuvred cautiously, and was soon able to saw away at the cord binding her arms. Soon it loosened enough for her to yank them apart, and Linda tore the gag out of her mouth and then, having waited for the agonising pins and needles in her arms to subside, she freed her ankles.

Stiffly she got to her feet. There was a small window, but it gave her only a limited view of the farmyard and barns, set a good distance away behind and to one side of the main house. She turned to the door. Surely Pete and his men would be too busy in the main part of the house to notice her moving around.

They could even be gone. They'd surely want to move as fast as possible.

How long had she been here? The event had just started, at half past one, when she had been captured. She glanced at her watch, then shook it. Surely it could not be only half past two? It seemed like hours since she'd come rushing round the house and seen them preparing to break in.

She'd tuned out the noise of the loudspeaker but it could be heard clearly. Now she heard the announcer explaining the development of bows and saying they were to see several types in this display. That had been due to start at two-thirty, she recalled.

The parade and the jousting would be over. But she still had to escape from this room.

She tried the door, rattling it in her frustration, and heard a dull thud outside. For a moment she didn't recognise the sound, then she realised it was the key which had fallen out of the lock. Linda kneeled down and inspected the bottom of the door. The floorboards had warped slightly, and if the key hadn't fallen too far away, she could fish it through the gap, and would be able to get out.

She looked at the weaponry stored all around, and decided to try a sword. Carefully abstracting one from the umbrella stand, and drawing it from the scabbard, she poked the blade beneath the door. It was thicker than she'd expected, and the hilt made it impossible to lay it flat, so that idea was a non-starter.

She replaced the sword, inspected several others to find they were no more suitable, and then decided to try an arrow.

This was far better, and after some tricky moments Linda was able to pull the key beneath the door. Heaving a sigh of relief she stood up and inserted it in the lock. It turned smoothly, indicating that the key was used often and the lock oiled.

Linda looked out cautiously, but saw

and heard nothing. She went into a room on the opposite side and craned to see into the courtyard. One of the horse boxes was still there, but the one Pete had been standing on had gone. That probably meant he had gone, too.

Still taking every precaution not to make a noise, Linda crept down the stairs.

Had Pete stolen the miniatures? She had to find out.

On the lower floor she got her bearings and moved slowly along towards the rooms where they had been before. There were no other sounds. The house was eerily quiet.

4

In the Great Hall, where light came in only through some windows high in the wall, there were deep shadows, and it was astonishingly cool. She edged round the room, ready to dive into hiding behind the heavy oak furniture if anyone appeared. Finally, she reached the newest section of the house. This was the door into the main drawing room, where the miniatures were displayed.

She opened it and looked inside. There was no-one there, but there were also no pictures, and the doors of the display cabinets where the porcelain and silver had been housed swung open. Pete had taken more than the miniatures. Linda moved into the room and stared round in dismay. What else had he taken from other rooms? Then a noise caused her to spin round in alarm, her heart racing with fear.

'You should have left with your friends, my child, or were you about to telephone for assistance?'

He was tall, dark-eyed with short fair hair, and familiar. Instead of his armour and surcoat, he wore brief white shorts and a skimpy T-shirt, which showed the muscles of his bronzed legs and arms and left little to the imagination. Linda swallowed.

'Who, who are you?' she managed to croak when her breath returned.

'Ladies first, your name and an explanation of what you are doing in private property which has, apparently, been stripped of many valuables,' he replied, a grim smile on his lips.

'I'm Linda Slater, and I was caught and imprisoned by the men who did this,' she said slowly.

It sounded so melodramatic. Things like that didn't just happen, but they had happened, to her.

'We must phone the police,' she added.

'Don't worry, they know. No doubt you'll be answering their questions soon.'

'How can they know? Who told them? Have they been caught?' she demanded, her hopes rising.

'No, they haven't been caught, unfortunately. I phoned the police, as soon as I realised the security system had been tampered with. By the way, I'm Simon Cottrell. My father owns The Old Grange.'

'They went off in a horse box,' Linda said slowly. 'It was in the courtyard at the back. Pete, one of the men, was on top doing something to the security box on the wall when I found them.'

He regarded her with raised eyebrows.

'Have you decided to tell on them?'

'You think I was part of the gang?' Linda demanded indignantly, understanding his hints.

'Aren't you? How do you know their names?'

'I came here with Pete today. We

— we've been seeing one another for the past few weeks,' Linda said slowly. 'But I had no idea he was a thief. How could I?' she demanded.

'Well, I might believe you,' he said slowly.

'Might!' Linda said, furious. 'I'm telling you the truth, and if you don't believe me you can come and see where I left the cords and rags they used to tie me up!'

Without waiting for his reaction, Linda sped from the room, taking him by surprise. She was halfway across the Great Hall before he caught up with her. He grasped her arm and swung her round so that she stumbled and fell against his chest.

'It's true! Let me go!' she gasped, sudden panic making her tremble.

She'd had enough of being manhandled by large men, and for a moment feared he meant to imprison her, too.

'Just calm down. Where were you going?'

'The room in the old part, where there are lots of suits of armour,' she explained. 'They tied me up and gagged me, and left me there, locked in. I escaped.'

He regarded her with a mixture of amusement and suspicion in his eyes.

'Don't you believe me?'

She wriggled round to look over her shoulder.

'Look, I tore my T-shirt on a nail, and cut my arm using it to cut the cords. Luckily they were only thin ones, and not very strong.'

He lifted her hands and studied the scratches and traces of dried blood on her wrists.

'Come with me. These need attention.'

Without giving her time to protest, he took her hand and led the way back through the drawing room, out of a door at one end, and up a flight of stairs. Along a passage he entered a large bedroom whose windows over-looked the front of the house, and Linda suddenly realised the events outside were still continuing. The loudspeaker was clearer here, and now announcing the Battle of Lewes.

'Oh, blast, I am supposed to be taking part in this. Well, they'll have to do without me,' he exclaimed.

Linda felt absurdly guilty, and began to apologise. He laughed.

'Don't worry. I'll survive, and so will they.'

Simon Cottrell led the way through the bedroom and into a spacious bathroom.

'Sit on the stool, and tell me what happened,' he said as he opened a small cabinet and took out ointment and plasters.

He was beginning to believe her, thank goodness. Linda took a deep breath and began to explain. As he took her hands and washed the scratches, she flinched, but it was more from the feel of his warm hands on hers than the sting of the wounds. She forced herself to concentrate on essentials, explaining how Pete had expected her to help, how she'd refused, and tried to stop him, but been caught instead.

'Were they wearing gloves?' he asked, pressing a plaster over one of the scratches that was still slightly oozing blood.

'Not that I could see.'

'Then later you can show the police exactly where this fellow took you. Did he open doors?'

'Yes,' she recalled. 'He opened several until he found the room where he left me.'

'Then we'd best not disturb that now. He may have left fingerprints or other traces the police could analyse and might use to identify him. Can you describe them? And where does this Pete live, your boyfriend? Do you know?'

'He's not my boyfriend!' Linda protested.

Her feelings for Pete had suffered such a reversal she didn't want to think about how much she'd liked him until today. Simon moved behind her and Linda twisted round to watch him. He was regarding the tear in her T-shirt.

'Take this off. You've blood on your back.'

'Take off my T-shirt?' she demanded indignantly. 'No thanks. It's no more than a little scratch.'

He grinned suddenly.

'As you wish. You can preserve your modesty, though I've no evil intentions. You needn't worry I'm about to attack you. I've better things to do, such as trying to find those thieving friends of yours.'

She fumed. Did he believe her or not? He'd appeared to accept her explanation, but now he was referring to her friends as though he still thought she was part of the gang.

'Come on. The police will be here by now.'

She followed him downstairs and through a door at the back of the Great Hall into the courtyard. Several police cars had arrived and men were examining the ground and the broken window. A man in jeans and a lightweight anorak walked across to them.

'I'm Inspector Stone, in charge. Stay here, please, Mr Cottrell, miss. The scene-of-crime officers have work to do. I'd like to talk to you both, and anyone else who was around, later on.'

He turned away and Simon leaned against the wall.

'Who were you trying to telephone earlier?' he asked casually.

Linda glanced at him.

'Why? What does it have to do with this?' she asked in as controlled a voice as possible.

'I don't know, but you were in a rather frantic state. Who were you so desperate to contact?'

Linda thought swiftly. She was aware that some mobile phones stored numbers which had been dialled. She dared not lie.

'It was my brother, his flat and then his mobile,' she replied, turning to look enquiringly up into Simon's face. 'Why do you want to know?'

'Why the urgency?' he insisted.

'I'd had a row with Pete. I needed a

lift home, since I'd come with him. I wanted Bill to come and pick me up.'

'So quickly? Couldn't it have waited?'

'Why should it? I didn't want to stay and watch this play-acting on my own,' she snapped.

He chuckled.

'But then you decided to stay and try to prevent the burglary. Why did you decide to confront your boyfriend on your own instead of telling someone who could have brought in the police? There are several uniformed men controlling the traffic here.'

'I didn't think,' Linda said.

'No? Or perhaps you thought you didn't want your boyfriend caught. Is that it? You may have objected to the robbery, but I'm not entirely convinced of that. I believe you wanted to warn him, hoped maybe that he would be frightened off. Either that, or for some reason you're lying about being captured. Well, Linda Slater, you will have to stay here until we find out the truth.'

5

'You can't keep me here!' Linda protested to the young, fair-haired son of the present owner of The Old Grange.

'The police can,' he reminded her, and she bit her lip, looking up to see the man in jeans, who was in charge, was coming towards them.

'Mr Cottrell, is there a room we can use as a base to interview people?'

Simon nodded.

'There's the old dining room. It's next to the sitting room where they broke in, through that door in the corner, and the room before the disturbed one. There are plenty of chairs and tables. Shall I show you?'

'I can find it, thanks. I'll call you when we're ready.'

'I've discovered one room where pictures and silver and porcelain, I suspect, have been stolen. Do you want me to look around the rest of the house?'

'Not yet, if you please. Would you wait somewhere nearby and then I'll go round with you and make a list?'

'We'll wait in the Great Hall.'

Linda went back with him, knowing she had no alternative. Of course the police could detain her, and they would want to question her. Should she tell them about Jake? It would influence them against her if they discovered she had a cousin who was a small-time crook and had spent six months in prison for theft. On the other hand, if she did not tell them and they found out, it would make it look bad for her.

She wished she hadn't rung Bill from Simon Cottrell's phone, but it was too late for that. The story she had concocted would have to do, and it could have been true, she thought guiltily. When she'd been thinking straight she could well have phoned Bill to come and fetch her in his car.

Though she'd have been far more likely to have phoned her mother.

Simon was taking her arm. Was he afraid she'd try to run away? He moved across to the huge fireplace where there were bench seats actually inside the chimney. He gestured to her to sit down.

'I'm sorry we can't have a grandstand view of the re-enactments,' he said, 'but we can hear them from here.'

Linda had almost forgotten, but in this stone building the noise of the loudspeaker seemed louder.

'Will you be missed?' she asked. 'Are you taking part in other displays?'

'Trying to get rid of me?' he asked, and she flushed and shook her head. 'No, the jousting was over, luckily, and there are others who can take my place in the crowd scenes, the battles.'

'Why do you do it?'

He shrugged.

'I teach history at a college, and what better way of understanding how people of different ages felt than by trying to recreate some of their life? Also I ride, and this place is ideally laid out with the arena and the hill for people to sit and watch. It helps the finances, big events like this. The few people who come to see the house itself won't pay for its upkeep.'

'Pete said you and your brothers ran the farm and a stud,' she recalled out loud.

'Yes, my brothers do that, and I help during vacations. They have their own houses, some distance away from the main one. They don't live here. So your Pete had done his homework, had he?'

'He's not my Pete!'

'He was, I presume, until this morning. How long had you known him?'

'Just a few weeks. He said he'd been transferred to a new branch of his firm, so was new to the area. He did have a job. I telephoned him there and left messages occasionally. He's a computer engineer.'

'You'll have to tell this to the police.'

'I know. I thought he was interested in old buildings, and he seemed to know a lot about paintings. We went to some house or other almost every weekend.'

'Casing the joints, no doubt.'

Miserably Linda nodded. It did seem that way.

'Do you know where he lived? I don't suppose he went back there, but it might give the police some clues.'

'He had a flat, two rooms, really, in Bridge Street.'

He'd said he was going to look for a house, and had implied he wanted Linda to share it, but she would try to forget that. How could she have been so gullible?

'May I try to phone my brother now?' she asked tentatively.

Simon had his mobile attached to his belt.

'I don't think that would be a good idea,' he said. 'I'm sure the police would not like to think a possible witness has been warned.'

'Witness? But Bill knows nothing about this, and I'll need a lift home.'

'Either I or the police will take you home. As for Bill, he may or may not have knowledge of this, but it will make the police more suspicious if you do speak to him. Does he know Pete?'

Linda nodded, but did not add that Bill had introduced Pete to her. It would make it look even worse for her brother, though why should it, she asked herself angrily. Even crooks had to know some ordinary people, surely. Being acquainted with a thief didn't automatically make her one. She hadn't thought this way when Jake had been convicted, just been ashamed of being related.

Hours later, long after the outdoor events were finished and the crowds had departed, except for the performers who were staying in their tents, the police seemed satisfied. Linda felt drained. Their determined and skilful questioning had dragged from her more information than she had known she possessed about Pete Jackson. Men had been sent to his flat, to talk to Bill, and to find Jake.

While she was being questioned, Simon had attempted to list all the stolen items, though as he'd said to Linda, he couldn't remember the half of them. His father had the inventory in the safe, and he and Lady Cottrell wouldn't be home from a trip to Paris until Thursday.

'You can go home now, Miss Slater, and thank you for your co-operation.'

She hadn't heard more welcome words all day.

'I don't have a car,' she began to say, but Inspector Stone smiled.

In other circumstances she'd have liked him, she thought. He had a fatherly smile, but he'd shown his ruthless side during the questioning.

'Mr Cottrell is going to take you. He'll be here in a few minutes, he said.'

He left her then, and Linda slumped in the chair. She was exhausted, and the heat and stickiness of the day had combined with her bruises and the dust from that attic floor to make her feel thoroughly dishevelled.

When Simon came in, she saw enviously he had found time to shower and change into a clean shirt and jeans which clung to his muscular legs.

'Come on. I imagine you are ravenous. I'll take you to have some food at the local pub.'

'I can't go anywhere like this! I'm filthy, my shirt's torn, and my hair's a mess.'

'It's not the Ritz,' he said, laughing. 'But if you'd feel better I can take you to your flat and you can change, then we'll find somewhere nearby.'

She was too weary to argue, and meekly went with him to his car, housed in a large barn just beyond the walled garden. It was long, low and sleek, but she didn't know what make, and had almost fallen asleep by the time they reached the town and he had to ask the directions to her flat. Her shower revived her, and she gave her hair a quick blow dry. She didn't have time to ponder over what to wear, dragging the first thing to hand out of her wardrobe, a plain blue skirt that matched her eyes, and a white lacy blouse she'd brought back from holiday in Spain last year. A dab of lipgloss, a spray of perfume, and she was ready.

Simon knew of a small bistro nearby, and soon they were seated opposite each other. They avoided talk of the robbery over their meal, and Simon persuaded her to talk about her job in the head-hunting agency, while he told her of some of his students. Soon they were laughing easily, and as they rose to leave, Linda found herself wishing they had met in other circumstances.

They'd left his car by her flat and walked to the bistro, and as they strolled back in the balmy summer evening, still light enough to see clearly, Linda forced herself reluctantly to consider the events of the day, and their consequences.

'Will the police want to talk to me

again?' she asked abruptly, ignoring his comment about how quiet the neighbourhood was.

'I imagine so, but there's nothing to worry about if you've told them the truth.'

'I've told them everything I know.'

'Yes, but there may be small points you've forgotten. I think everyone does. It's difficult, in the stress of the moment, to recall everything. At least that's what my students tell me when they are excusing test failures.'

They'd reached the converted house where Linda had her flat, the basement floor with its own entrance down a short flight of steps.

'Will you come in for coffee?' she asked hesitantly.

'I won't stop, but I'll see you safely inside.'

She went down the steps in front of him, fishing for her keys in her bag, and then gasped in dismay. Her door was open, just a small gap showing.

'They've been here!' she gasped. 'I'll

kill Pete if he's trashed my flat!'

'Let me see,' Simon ordered, and before she could protest had thrust his way past her into the tiny hall.

Having had time to think that Pete or one of his bully boy friends might be lying in wait, Linda tried to grab his hand and hold him back, but she was too slow. She followed him in, and they went from the small sitting room which stretched across the entire back of the house, with french windows opening on to a small patio garden, into the tiny kitchen, the bedroom at the front, and the bathroom.

All the rooms were empty, the french windows were still secure, and nothing had been disturbed. Simon stood in the middle of the sitting room, looking round thoughtfully.

'What did they want?' he mused.

Linda, as puzzled as she was, went to fill the kettle and as she lifted it, gave a gasp. Below, concealed until then, was a small envelope. She picked it up and ripped open the flap. The note inside was brief and to the point.

Don't tell the police anything or you'll regret it.

Hours later Linda collapsed into bed. Simon had insisted on calling the police, and they had spent ages searching the flat and the gardens, and taking statements. Then there had been the argument about whether or not she could stay there.

'If you can go to your parents it would be best,' the policeman had said.

'I can't wake them up at this hour,' Linda protested. 'It's two in the morning!'

'You can come and stay at The Old Grange. That will be the most secure place in the area tonight,' Simon insisted, 'and I think you ought to stay there for a few more nights until the police have had time to catch the rogues.'

Eventually she had agreed and packed a small case with clothes for the following day, and her office clothes for Monday. Surely by then Pete would have been caught and she'd be safe. Simon had shown her to a room next to his own, also with an en suite bathroom, and promised she would not be woken too early in the morning.

'The re-enactors will be in their own tents, and as it's the second day they'll not have to set things out. You'll be able to sleep well into the morning.'

6

It was eleven before she woke, and for some moments she lay in blissful comfort, aware of the sun shining through gaps in the curtains, and faint noises from outside. They did not, however, sound like the traffic noises she was used to, and suddenly it all flooded back, the disaster of yesterday. Simon had shown her a bell rope, and told her to pull on it when she was ready.

'I'll be out, I expect,' he'd said, 'seeing to the horses and preparations for today, but Maggie, the housekeeper, will be here, and she'll show you where you can have breakfast and let me know you're ready. Then we can make sure you'll be safe during the day.'

She shivered, and decided to delay matters by soaking in a bath. The bathroom had a selection of essences, a pile of wonderfully soft towels, and the bath was deep enough for her to sink completely into the water. As she relaxed she began to plan.

Last night she'd been too shocked to want to think about it, but now she was growing angry. How dare Pete assume she was the sort of girl who'd join him in criminal activities! They'd all three treated her despicably, and she'd been terrified, but now she was just angry. Of course she was fearful, she'd be stupid not to be concerned at what they might do, especially when he realised, as he would, that the police knew who was responsible. But she wanted him as much as the police did, and she would do her best to ensure his capture.

Springing out of the bath, refreshed by her soak, she pulled on the clean jeans and shirt she had packed last night, then rang for Maggie. While she waited, she drew back the curtains and saw that she had an excellent view of the arena to the front of the house.

She heard a discreet knock on the

door and Maggie, a plump woman in her fifties, appeared.

'Hello, you're awake. Mr Simon said you might like breakfast up here, or if you want to come downstairs he'll join you.'

'I'll come downstairs, thanks,' Linda said. 'I'm sorry it's so late, but I slept far better than I expected to, after all the excitement.'

'Dreadful, isn't it? But I'm sure, with your help, the police will catch them. If you're ready then, I'll show you the way.'

Linda followed her down the main staircase and through to a surprisingly modern kitchen at the far end of the most modern wing.

'Do you mind eating there?' Maggie asked, indicating a huge, pine table at one end of the room, where cereals and a pot of coffee were already set out. 'Mr Simon always prefers it when his parents are away. Help yourself to coffee. It's a fresh pot.'

'Does he live here all the time?'

Linda asked, sitting down and reaching for cereal.

'Only in the vacation. He has a house near his college.'

There was no time for more, as Simon came in through a door leading to the knot garden courtyard.

'Good, I hope you slept well? You certainly look better than when we met.'

'I should hope so,' Linda replied, with a grimace at how she must have looked then. 'Coffee?'

'Please, and, Maggie, a full fry-up, I hope? No-one does breakfast better than Maggie,' he added. 'I don't indulge anywhere else, but I can't resist Maggie's sausages and bacon.'

Maggie, smiling, was already busy at the grill, and Simon turned back to Linda.

'How are we going to keep you safe today, just in case they come here looking for you?'

'Will they?' she asked. 'I hope they do, and I spot them first!'

'You could stay in the bedroom. No intruder will get in today with all the extra police we have around, and you'll have a good view of all the demonstrations from there. I have suggested to Dad that he should rent out the rooms overlooking the arena, like they do for processions in London, but he thinks that's too commercial!'

'No, I want to join in. I saw very little yesterday, but you told me so much I want to see it for myself.'

'But if Jackson goes to your flat, finds you've moved out, he may suspect you're back here. He may even think the police want you here, and he might come looking. Could you identify the other two?'

'Yes, I'm sure I could.'

'Good, but we don't want them recognising you. You'd better put on a disguise.'

'A disguise? Oh, you mean dress up as a re-enactor?'

'Yes. There are spare costumes. I keep them here for some groups, and if we can't find any that fit, the stall-holders have some for sale. They make them from authentic materials, and in the traditional way. You'd better be a mediaeval peasant. Their clothing is the most concealing, and you can wrap the wimple round your head to cover your hair.'

Linda knew he was right, but she felt a longing for the more elaborate Tudor dresses she'd seen yesterday, with their laces and jewels and embroidery, the low necklines and high ruffs. This dressing-up business had its points, she realised. She might enjoy it herself.

After a substantial breakfast, Simon vanished, saying he preferred to disguise her before she left the house.

Within minutes he was back with a girl her own age, but shorter, dressed in a drab green, floor-length gown, and carrying another in dark reddish brown over her arm.

'This is Eleanor,' he said. 'She'll show you how to put everything on, and

make sure you have comfortable sandals. Then she'll stay with you and show
you how to go on. You can use the
breakfast room just along the passage.'

He led the way, and deposited the
basket full of leather sandals and
lengths of white and fawn material on a
chair. He explained these were the
wimples which wrapped round their
heads and necks.

'I'd better go and get ready myself, or
someone else will have to do the
jousting, and there's no-one really
competent yet. I'll be around, Linda,
and there's also a policeman who'll be
dressed in peasant clothing who will
come with you and Eleanor.'

'It's good of you to help,' Linda said
as she stripped off her shirt and jeans
and Eleanor lifted the linen undergown
over her head.

'No problem. This one's the right
length, I think. Simon seemed to
know your measurements to the last
centimetre,' she added, grinning.

Linda blushed.

'Have you known him long?'

'About six years. I was one of his students, and he got me interested in all this, and a couple of years ago when I began to work near here, I joined the group.'

'What do you do?' Linda asked as Eleanor pulled on the blue gown.

'I'm in the police.'

'What?'

Linda spun round to find Eleanor grinning at her.

'You don't think Simon would give guard duty to someone unqualified to protect you?'

'I hadn't considered it. But you're shorter than I am, and I bet I'm a lot heavier.'

'But you haven't been trained in judo.'

Suddenly Linda collapsed with laughter.

'I'd love to see Pete or one of those other beasts take a fall from a mediaeval judo expert half their size!'

'Let's hope they do. If I throw one, you can sit on him until help comes.'

Eleanor draped the wimple round Linda's head, and Linda was surprised to find how comfortable the whole outfit was. She put on a pair of thonged sandals, and Eleanor made her walk up and down the room until she was comfortable in her flowing skirts.

'Right, you'll do. David, or to give him his proper title, Sergeant David Evans, will be waiting for us outside. There's an hour before we have to prepare for the parade, so let's go and I'll introduce you to the rest of the group up at the camp. We might even set you to spinning or stirring the cauldron.'

'I can't spin,' Linda said in horror.

'You can hold a spindle, but most of the time Simon wants us to wander round amongst the crowd, for you to try to spot Pete or the others.'

'And I hope they're here!' Linda said feelingly.

7

'The programme's the same as yester-day's,' Eleanor said as she and Linda, with David Evans on Linda's other side, wandered through the crowds already staking their claims to good viewing and picnic spots. 'I wish you had a photo of Pete, then I could be looking for him, too. The police didn't find anything at his flat.'

'That's been searched?' Linda asked.

Her lingering hope that Pete would not know the police were aware of his involvement died. He'd be even more determined to find her.

'It was searched last night, but there wasn't even a passport, and almost no personal papers,' David told her.

'So he'll know the police have been there.'

'Yes. We don't know if he knew that before or after he left that note for you, but my guess is before, or he'd have worded it differently. I imagine he'd have been occupied for several hours hiding what he took from here. And if he went home while we were there, he might have come back and kept watch on you, seen you with Simon. He might even have been intending to do something then.'

'Take revenge, you mean?' Linda shivered. 'He never came out well in photos,' she went on thoughtfully. 'Not that I took many, just a couple when we were out with some other people. He always moved or turned away at the wrong moment.'

'Or the right one,' Eleanor commented.

'You mean, it was deliberate?' Linda said.

'Probably. We've checked him out,' David said. 'He's got a real job, but he had a record of petty theft when he was a juvenile, in Bristol. Nothing in the past ten years, and the last probation report from Bristol was optimistic he'd turned over a new leaf, was studying hard and applying to colleges. After that noone seems to have known anything.'

'When he was planning bigger thefts,' Linda said angrily. 'It's a wonder he didn't concentrate on computer fraud.'

'Well, according to his previous boss, he's not actually all that good with computers. He's really just a salesman. Knows enough to convince the buyers they're getting what suits them, but none of the really clever stuff.'

They walked on for a while, scanning the faces of spectators, and then Linda sighed.

'It's impossible! There must be two or three thousand people here already, and there's half an hour to go before the parade, and I can't really believe he'd be fool enough to come back here. In his shoes I'd get as far away as I could.'

David laughed.

'But you're not a macho crook, and some of them can be amazingly stupid. That's why they get caught.'

'And not because the police are so much cleverer?' Linda asked, grinning.

'We hope we are! I think we'd better go back and get into position for the parade,' Eleanor said, turning round.

'Parade? Me? But I'm nothing to do with this!'

'Linda, for today you are a member of a re-enactment society, and if we stayed out of the parade, dressed as we are, we'd cause comment. All we have to do is walk along with the rest of them. Later we can mix in the crowds, watching again.'

Behind the house, several hundred re-enactors were milling about, forming into groups, being marshalled by stewards into the right order for the procession. At the front were eight boldly-adorned horses, dressed for the tournament, and Simon was mounted on one with the same green and scarlet livery he'd worn the previous day. As Linda lifted her hand to wave, Eleanor caught it and shook her.

'Don't show you know. It might give

you away,' she hissed. 'Pete or the others could be watching round here and they probably know Simon by sight.'

'Sorry.'

Linda bowed her head, trying to pull her wimple farther over her face.

The participants sorted themselves out, and at last the procession moved off. Linda's group was one of the first, and she and Eleanor, with David still close by, placed themselves in the middle of a group, some carrying pikes, others bows, and many clubs or baskets, and moved off to walk through the arena.

Linda began to enjoy herself. Ahead she could see Simon with the other horsemen, and for the first time she gave a thought to what would happen when all this was over. Pete would be caught, she had to believe that, but would Simon then disappear from her life? How could he, an academic who also bred horses and lived in a minor stately home, have anything in common with her? But she could recall every small thing about him, and knew she would never forget him. She'd imagined she liked Pete. He was good company, but she hadn't even begun to fall in love with him, and she'd never contemplated spending the rest of her life with him. With Simon, however, she'd felt at home.

Telling herself not to be silly, Linda tried to distract her thoughts by imagining what life would have been like in the twelfth or thirteenth centuries. The clothes were of wool and hot. She supposed that this warmth would be necessary in huts or houses with only a small cooking fire, but surely they'd have been difficult to wash, and soon become stale from sweat, smoke and the odours of cooking. On the whole she thought she was glad she lived when she did.

They had walked right round the house and once out of sight of the crowds, the various groups were dispersing. Linda stepped aside to watch, admiring the discipline with which the next group, a troop of soldiers, marched along. Several groups, peasants and soldiers and courtiers, passed by, and then came a laughing band of Tudor ladies and gentlemen. Behind them was the last group, more soldiers carrying long pikes, and as she glanced at them Linda froze.

'That's Pete!' she gasped, clutching Eleanor's hand. 'There, the tall, dark one in the last row, towards the far side. And I'm sure that's one of the other men, next to him. How on earth did he get involved?'

'I'll follow him. This lot won't be on until almost the end, the Battle of Flodden, and he could go anywhere,' David said, and moved away from them, seemingly aimlessly.

'We'll go and alert the boss,' Eleanor said, and Linda, speculation racing through her mind, automatically followed.

8

The police were still using the old dining room in the house. Simon had not wanted extra police cars or an official caravan incident room, all of which would publicise the theft, and if the public knew about it the police would have found it impossible to keep gawpers away from the back of the house.

There were several plain clothes policemen and policewomen mingling with the crowds, all equipped with mobile phones, and after Eleanor's report, several of these were sent to the living history areas in case Pete had gone there.

'We'll go and see. I know some of them. I'll try to find out how he got involved,' Eleanor said.

'We must tell Simon!' Linda insisted. 'Pete may be after him, too.'

'Simon's in the jousting right now, but he'll be told as soon as that's finished.'

Eleanor and Linda walked through the crowds, and despite Linda's urging, Eleanor refused to hurry.

'You might give him warning,' she said, holding Linda's arm and forcing her to halt. 'We must behave naturally, and you must watch Simon. He's brilliant at this.'

In the arena, they had set up a low fence, and Simon was circling round at one end, a long lance in one hand, shield in the other. Opposite, garbed in brilliant blue and yellow, was another mounted knight. At a signal, the two horses wheeled and raced towards one another, one either side of the fence, lances raised.

'They will try to hit one another,' Eleanor was explaining rapidly, just as the horses came level, the fence between them. 'They have a points system of scoring. Oh, well done!'

Simon was galloping on, lance held

aloft, while his opponent carried a much shortened lance.

'He broke it?'

'Yes, and that's a high score. Come on, time to move a bit farther.'

Linda would have liked to stay. It had been such a thrill watching Simon triumph, but there were more serious matters to deal with. She followed Eleanor through the crowds towards the tent areas. Many of these were brightly coloured, flags flying on top, and she recalled seeing pictures in history books of such pavilions. Eleanor stopped in the shelter of one of them and pulled a mobile phone out of the basket she still carried. Turning away so that this incongruous sight would not be seen, she spoke softly into it, then listened.

'Pete is wandering round the stalls, very interested in the replica weapons,' Eleanor reported efficiently. 'David's waiting for reinforcements and then they'll arrest Pete. I'll try and find the people I know while he's safely out of the way, maybe discover who knows him, and whether his pals are here, too.'

Linda, worried about Pete's intentions, would have preferred to go to him and make sure the police captured him, but Eleanor pointed out she might frighten him away if he recognised her.

'You have to be discreet, ready to turn away if we see him. Or worse, he might attack you.'

'Not in a crowd. He'd never get away with it.'

'Lots of attacks take place in crowds. They conceal people. He's being watched.'

Linda had to accept Eleanor's advice, but they spent the next half an hour fruitlessly asking questions. No-one amongst the Tudor soldiers knew Pete, or recognised him from Linda's description.

'We're two groups today,' one of Eleanor's friends explained, 'so there are plenty of people we don't know. We needed to make up the numbers for the battle, see.'

'What now?' Linda asked.

'Back to base, I think, and see whether they've caught him,' Eleanor replied.

The archery display was taking place as they went back to the house, and they paused for a few moments, but both were eager to know what was happening.

As they rounded the Great Hall into the courtyard, Simon was coming the other way, and Linda ran across to meet him.

'He's here, in Tudor costume,' she said hurriedly.

Simon put his arm round her shoulders.

'This armour!' he complained. 'A metal hug isn't exactly pleasant, but I have to keep it on for the battles. Have they arrested him?'

'We're about to see,' Eleanor said, leading the way into the house.

A furious Inspector Stone was shouting into the telephone when they entered the dining room. He flung it down on the table and swung round to them.

'The fools, they let him go!'

'How?' Eleanor asked. 'David was with him, just waiting for some backup.'

'He went into one of the tents which sold costumes, and as Evans reports it, must have slid out between the flaps at the back. They weren't tied down or fixed together. He probably took one of the cloaks, because when Evans realised what had happened they couldn't see any Tudor costumes, only two or three people almost completely hidden by ankle-length cloaks!'

'That settles it. You'll stay inside the house for the rest of the afternoon, Linda,' Simon said.

'But I'm the only one who can identify him!'

'And he, as well as the fellow with him, can identify you. They can only have come here in order to find you, prevent you from giving evidence. I want you out of harm's way.'

Before she could argue, the inspector chimed in.

'He's right, miss. We'd rather get him

for theft than murder.'

'You're not likely to get him at all unless I help you.'

'You have helped. You've narrowed the field, and we can concentrate on Tudor soldiers.'

'Maggie will be in the kitchen, and she'll see you have everything you want,' Simon told her. 'I suggest you watch from the bedroom. You can lock that door, and you'll be perfectly safe.'

She protested, but they were all against her. Simon brusquely informed her that he had to get ready for the next event, where he was taking part. Reluctant, plotting how she would escape, Linda permitted him to escort her upstairs.

'Ring for Maggie if you want anything,' he said as he almost pushed her in the room, and before she could reply he had gone.

Linda was thinking furiously. Since various pieces of armour had been stored up in the attic room where she had been imprisoned, it was possible there was other clothing, too, which she could use. Simon said he helped various of the societies who used the Grange for events by storing their surplus gear. That was probably where Eleanor had found the clothes she wore now.

Impatient, she waited by the window until the footsoldiers and horsemen who were taking part in the Battle of Lewes appeared on the arena. She ought to be able to move around the house unseen now.

Cautiously she opened the door and peered out. Silence greeted her. Sliding out, she wondered if she had to go down and across the Great Hall, or if there was another way of getting into the oldest part of the house. She recalled a minstrels' gallery, across the front of the Great Hall, and hoped there were doors connecting that to the other wings. She'd seen no stairs to it from the Great Hall itself.

It took a frustrating fifteen minutes of opening doors and exploring various passages before she succeeded. A door she'd suspected might be just another cupboard led through into the gallery, and at the far side she saw a matching door.

Breathing a sigh of relief she continued on, and soon found her way up to the attics. First she tried the room where she had been held the previous day, shuddering at the memory, but there was only the armour she'd seen and the weapons.

In the next room, however, she found what she wanted. There were several dress rails, and hanging on them a variety of historical costumes, each, she was thankful to see, with a ticket attached which gave the date.

She paused. It was imperative her head was covered, her fair hair was far too recognisable, so her first ploy to dress as a man was difficult. She was considering a monk's habit when her eye was caught by a short, hooded cape.

The hood had a long point, but

would cover her hair, and there was a knee-length tunic and green hose with it. Late thirteenth century, the ticket said.

Linda stripped off her long gown and the wimple, and struggled into the new garments. The tunic was too big for her, but she was able to pull it tight with the belt. In a cupboard she found boxes of shoes, and chose a comfortable pair of soft leather, ankle height.

Now she had to get out of the house unseen. She decided it would be safer to go through the old wing, as the police were constantly coming and going to their headquarters in the old dining room. With luck, anyone who saw her would imagine she was a witness come to give them some information.

The Battle of Lewes, she'd discovered when talking to Simon the previous night, was well before Tudor times, so Pete was not likely to be involved, but he could be planning to join in the later battle, Flodden.

Simon and the other horsemen were in all of them as well as the jousting, changing their armour and other costumes to the appropriate ones of the time, and she was beginning to worry that part of Pete's plan was to injure Simon. He'd probably been watching her flat, and would have seen them together.

Thankful that this older building had very small windows, and dark passages, she went down the stairs carefully, and paused when she heard the inspector's voice raised.

He was haranguing David, she realised, calling him all sorts of a fool to let Jackson slip away from him.

Poor David, she thought, but at least it was occupying their attention.

She walked as nonchalantly as she could through into the courtyard, and tried to look preoccupied as she strolled across.

Once out of sight, she quickened her steps, and made for the living history tents. Pete was most likely to be there, she'd decided, waiting his moment.

The Battle of Lewes was coming to an end, according to the loudspeaker commentary. She hurried past, glancing across to the arena to see the supposedly wounded and killed soldiers picking themselves up and walking after their comrades.

The horsemen had left, and she wondered whether Simon would check on her during the falconry display. Well, it was too late. He shouldn't have treated her like a child.

The Tudor tents were at the far side of the living history area, right up against the field boundary hedge, and as she drew nearer, Linda could see modern caravans in the adjacent field.

So the participants didn't sleep on the ground as their forebears had, she thought with a slight smile.

She slowed, looking about her for signs of Pete or his cronies. There were several people demonstrating crafts, a young girl at a spinning wheel, a smith at an anvil, a woman dipping rushes into fat to make candles, a man making shoes, two women explaining what was in the dishes laid out as if for a banquet. She stopped to ask if they knew where Pete was, describing him briefly.

She'd seen several women dressed as soldiers, presumably to make up the numbers, so there was no need to disguise her voice. There was no information, though.

Linda was standing at the end of the row of tents, wondering what to do next, when she heard cries of alarm and indignant shouts behind her. She glanced up to see a horseman galloping along the path between the tents, and her eyes widened in dismay. She moved hastily out of his path, but he reined the horse to a halt, leaped from the saddle, and tossed the reins to a man standing by.

'Hold him for a moment, if you will,' he said, and Linda recognised Simon, a very angry Simon, bearing down on her.

He'd dispensed with his armour, and wore jeans and a T-shirt.

'You little idiot!' he snapped, seizing her arm in a punishing grip. 'I told you to stay put!'

'And just who are you to give me orders?' Linda gasped, breathless both from his sudden appearance, and the speed with which he was dragging her into the nearest pavilion.

'The police gave you orders, too,' he snapped, both hands now on her shoulders. 'But they slipped up, letting you escape.'

'How did you know me?' she demanded, her teeth chattering as he shook her.

'The house has security cameras,' he explained, his tone full of exasperation.

'Oh. Then you mean they watched me all the time?' Linda demanded indignantly.

'Yes, while you were in the corridors. They were a bit confused at first, to see someone in a different costume, and I gather all attention was on the inspector bawling out poor Evans, but they soon realised what had happened, and that was when I arrived there. I guessed where you'd be. Thank goodness you didn't find him. Or is it all a ploy? Are you being planted in the house in case there's an opportunity to get what they had to leave behind yesterday? Are you part of the gang, Linda?'

9

Linda, aghast, began to protest and tried to escape Simon's clutches, but he was speaking again.

'Whether you are involved or not can be decided later. For now you're coming back to the house with me. Luckily you don't have to manage a long gown. You can sit in front of me.'

She glanced across to the horse, and found several people, both in costume and spectators, listening eagerly to their confrontation. Argument would get her nowhere, she realised.

'OK then, but once back there I won't be bullied and shut out of the way for your convenience. I want to know what's going on.'

Wordlessly Simon, still grasping her arm firmly, led her across to where his horse waited. Seizing her round the waist he hoisted her into the saddle, and Linda hastily grabbed the pommel. Simon vaulted up behind her and briefly thanked the man who held the reins. Pulling them either side of Linda, he briefly ordered her to hang on and turned away from the tents.

'Where are we going?' she demanded, her voice shaking with mingled anger and something else she could not define.

He was so close to her she could feel his chest moving as he breathed, and feel his breath on her neck when he spoke.

'The house is the other way,' she said.

'We'll go through the caravan field. I upset enough people galloping through their camp ground. Let's not annoy them further. Besides, I'd have thought you would prefer to be less conspicuous. We still haven't traced Jackson yet.'

He was guiding the horse past a long row of caravans, cars and a variety of vans and even a couple of small horse boxes. Linda scanned the latter eagerly, but they were not the ones Pete had been using yesterday. They were about halfway down the row when something landed on the grass in front of them, causing the horse to throw up his head in alarm. Then whatever it was appeared to explode in a series of fizzing sparks. Linda realised it was a firework, one of the kind that jumped about in haphazard fashion, hissing and ejecting tiny flames.

It was too much for the horse. It reared and swerved, and Simon, though he clung desperately to the animal's flanks, could not keep his seat. He slid to the ground, and Linda, without his arms holding her, found herself falling sideways. She braced herself to hit the ground, but instead collided with a human body.

'Got you!' Pete crowed. 'Let the horse go,' he said in a louder voice, and Linda, struggling to turn away from the fierce clasp which bound her to his chest, saw two brawny men grabbing Simon and yanking him to his feet.

Then she was thrust through the

small door of a caravan, and thrown roughly on to the bench seat. Only the table beside it stopped her from falling on to the floor, but she was uncomfortably wedged, unable to sit upright. Outside she heard sounds of a struggle, some panting and cursing, then a door was slammed and a chain rattled.

'OK, boss, he's safe,' someone called, and she recognised the voice of the man who had carried her upstairs the day before.

Was it only twenty-four hours ago? Weeks seemed to have elapsed. And now Pete was standing, no longer in his Tudor costume, but dressed in jeans and a long-sleeved sweater, hands on hips, smirking down at her.

'Right, my lovely, first you can tell me all you told the police.'

'Find out.'

Linda felt it was a childish reply, but things had happened so rapidly, and she'd bumped her head on the table as she'd been thrown on to the bench, and couldn't think clearly.

'Where's Simon?' she asked.

'You tell me what I want to know and you can go and join lover-boy.'

Linda compressed her lips. She would not satisfy him. In any case, what could Pete do? The police would miss them, especially when the riderless horse was found, and there would be a search. At the very least, all vehicles would be searched before they were allowed to leave the site. Surely they would do that?

As the thoughts formed, the caravan was jolted, and she slid farther against the end wall. The levelling supports had been moved, and moments later a car engine burst into life, and the caravan rocked forward. Pete had thought ahead and planned this. Presumably one of his accomplices was driving.

There would be people on the exit, surely! There had been stewards directing the traffic to the parking areas when she'd first arrived and they had still been there when she and Simon had left the previous evening. She could shout for help. But once more Pete was ahead of her. Hauling her upright he once more gagged her.

'Once we're in a nice, quiet spot you can tell me all about it,' he said, grinning at her futile struggles, capturing her hands and tying them behind her back. 'Now lie down. It's illegal to travel in a towed caravan, you know. We don't want your police buddies to spot us, so we'll lie down all peaceful and keep mum until we're out of here.'

An hour later, the caravan rocked to a halt. Linda could see trees all round, but the only sound she heard was another vehicle, and through one of the big windows she saw a small horse box pull up beside them. Part of her felt relief that Simon was with her, then she felt guilty that he had been dragged into this fiasco through her stupidity. If she hadn't disobeyed orders and escaped from the house neither of them would have been kidnapped.

'Now, my pretty one, you'll tell me all,' Pete said, pulling her to a sitting position and untying the gag, before dragging her outside.

Linda saw, through the gloom of the windowless horse box, Simon sitting in a corner with his ankles bound and his arms, also presumably secured, behind his back. He had a livid bruise on one cheek, and blood had trickled from a cut on his forehead. Pete thrust her inside and as she fell on to her knees she heard the slam of the ramp which formed the door, and the bolts which held it in place being slammed home. This left a gap wide enough for a horse to hang his head out, but as she began to hope this would allow them to escape, if only they could get free of their bonds, two narrow lengths of wood were nailed roughly across it.

Then she heard a car start, and drive away. All she could see through the small gaps left were patches of sky and the topmost branches of a tree. Rolling over into a sitting position, bracing her back against the horse box wall, she looked at Simon.

'Simon, are you badly hurt?' she asked. 'I'm so dreadfully sorry. It's all my fault.'

'I should have left you to be hauled off like this on your own, should I?' he asked, and his contemptuous tone made her shrivel inside.

He was furious with her, and no wonder. It was all due to her crass stupidity they were in this jam. She swallowed, and said no more. At least she had the satisfaction of knowing she had told Pete nothing. He'd wanted to know what the police planned, how much she had told them about him, whether she could recognise and identify the other two men, who else he'd known, and where they'd been, especially the pubs, restaurants, and houses they'd visited.

After a few minutes Simon moved, sitting more upright.

'I'm sorry, Linda. Recriminations won't help. Perhaps now there are two of us we can at least undo these cords.'

'Sure,' she replied listlessly. 'But how can we get out of this contraption?'

'We'll figure that out when we're free. If we sit back to back, one of us might have enough movement in our fingers to undo the other one's knots.'

It took considerable manoeuvring before they could get into position, and both of them were sneezing from the dust disturbed from the layer of straw on the floor, but at last they sat in a position where Linda, whose hands seemed to have been less tightly bound, could set to work.

It was frustrating and tedious, especially as she had to work blind, but at last she loosened the knots sufficiently for Simon to get his hands free. He rubbed the circulation back into them, and Linda, twisting round to look, gasped in horror at the red weals where the cords had bit in to his flesh.

'The brutes! How could they tie them so tightly!'

'They didn't intend me to escape. It

was your good fortune they were less vicious with you.'

'Pete clearly either hasn't the same expertise as the others, or is less brutal,' Linda said.

'Or lover-boy put you here for some purpose of his own. Give me a moment to untie my legs, or I might lose my feet! Then I'll free you.'

Linda glared at him. The light was fading now, but enough light came through the small gaps to let her see his face.

'How can you still believe I'm in league with Pete after the way he treated me? What could he possibly hope for by chucking me in with you?'

'A passage into The Old Grange? Someone on the inside? When I took you back there last night he might have thought I'd been sufficiently attracted to you to give you free run of the place, which could have been useful for the things he didn't manage to remove the first time. In case you didn't know it, he missed some of the real treasures, though he'd started to take other less valuable items in the same cabinets.'

'Well, he didn't put me in here to spy on you,' she said angrily.

'As you say. Let me untie you now.'

10

Soon she was free and flexing her muscles. She hurt badly enough herself, but Simon must be in agony. She made it across to the back of the horse box and peered out. They were in a clearing, but it seemed to be in the middle of a densely-wooded area, one which had not been managed very well, for thick, tangled undergrowth and several dead and fallen trees covered the whole visible area.

Linda pushed the wooden bars, but they wouldn't budge. She glanced round their prison. Apart from the straw there was nothing else, nothing that could be used as a lever or battering ram to try and pry loose the planks. Simon came up beside her, and she flinched away from the touch of his warm arm against hers. She'd liked him so much and they'd got on so well the previous evening. His friendliness, his admiration, had to some extent restored her self-esteem after the shock of discovering Pete's true nature.

'Linda, I'm sorry,' Simon said suddenly, putting his arm round her shoulder and hugging her. 'I don't know what to think, and I'm furious with myself for allowing that crook to get the better of me. You must admit that as his girlfriend it looked suspicious, especially when you wouldn't stay put, and instead went off to try and find him.'

'I was not his girlfriend!' she insisted. 'I'd been out with him a few times, that's all. And I went out today because I was the only one who could identify him. I didn't expect him to have all this set up, or you to come after me like that.'

Simon pulled her closer, and she relaxed against him.

'It was Jackson's good fortune that I decided to go back to the house the more discreet way,' he admitted. 'If I'd stayed in the living history encampment he couldn't have caught us. But like you, I didn't think he'd attack us unless he was cornered. He's obviously deeper into criminal activities than we thought. I wonder . . . '

He paused, and absently stroked her arm, turning her to face him. Linda trembled. His closeness was doing things to her heart rate, and she was suddenly unable to breathe properly.

'Wonder what?' she asked, and her voice came out in a gasp.

'I wonder if some of the thefts from other country houses are connected,' he said slowly, and now both arms were round her and he was pulling her close to him.

Then Linda's heart performed acrobatics, for he smiled down at her and lowered his lips to hers.

'I can't really believe you and he are in cahoots,' he whispered, and captured her lips with his.

It was some time later when they once more faced the problem of what they could do to escape. By now the light had almost gone, and only a faint blur of lighter shapes revealed the gaps between the wooden bars.

'I'll have to try brute force,' Simon decided.

First he pushed as hard as he could on each length of wood, first one side, then the other, but none of them moved. He began to test each point where nails had been driven into the planks.

'I can get my hand out, but only so far. Your arms are slimmer, Linda. Can you reach through and feel if the nails are in firmly?'

Linda tried, but Simon had to lift her and support her before she could reach some of the nails. Eventually she gave a cry of triumph.

'This one's not fully home, and I can rock it slightly. Hold me steady, and I'll see if I can shift it.'

It took time, and it was fully dark by the time the nail came loose. Simon set her on her feet and pushed that end of the plank loose. Then he began to push and twist it, trying to loosen the nail on the other side, and eventually managed to prise the plank away. Carefully he pulled it inside and used it as a lever against the other one, but it stubbornly refused to give way. Simon paused for a rest, and Linda looked out of the gap, and then felt all round.

'Simon, are there just bolts at the top of the ramp, to hold it in place?'

'Probably. Why, can you reach them? I couldn't, and my arms are longer.'

'No, but I think I could get my head and shoulders out of this gap, if you hold me, and perhaps I could reach them then.'

'Let's try. They say if you can get your head through a space you can get the rest of your body through, too.'

'Do they? Well, I don't want to fall head first on the ground. Let's see if this works first.'

It was a struggle, and Linda scraped her shoulder on the plank above, but she managed to reach the bolts, and with a sigh of relief she almost fell out of the horse box as the ramp crashed to the ground.

'Quick, let's get out of here in case they're still around,' Simon said as they ran down it, and grabbed her hand.

Linda glanced across the clearing, and to her dismay saw the caravan and one car on the far side. A faint light glowed through the window of the caravan, and she needed no further urging to run as fast as she could for the shelter of the trees and the thick tangle of undergrowth. Simon pulled her down into a hollow behind a large tree trunk.

'I think they'd have heard us if they were still there,' he whispered in her ear. 'I expect they've gone for a meal, or to finish off something, such as hiding the loot. But the light indicates they mean to come back.'

'Not yet. I'm going to bolt the ramp and try to stick the plank back in place. Unless they look at us when they come back tonight, which I doubt, that will give us until morning before they realise we're gone.'

'I'll help then,' Linda said, though she wanted nothing more than to get as far away as they could, as quickly as possible. 'It'll be quicker.'

Together they crept back, raised the ramp and bolted it in place, and then fixed the plank roughly in place.

'Now we'll remove their car,' Simon said cheerfully.

'Steal it?' Linda asked. 'How?'

'They can't be here, so I'll break a window if it's locked, and luckily I was once shown how to start a car without a key.'

First they had to unhitch the caravan, and when it listed to one side Linda was finally convinced there was no-one else around. Simon found a short, stout branch and broke the driver's window, and soon he was driving along a narrow track which led out of the clearing.

'Let's hope they don't come back and block us in,' he said, and Linda wondered how he could be so cheerful in such a desperate situation. 'If they do, if we meet any other vehicle, dive out and run for it,' he ordered.

To her immense relief, after what seemed hours, they left the trees behind, and after a short stretch across an open field, the track ended at a narrow road. To the left was a glow of lights which appeared to be a road junction, so Simon turned that way.

'Soon, let's hope, we'll know where we are and be able to get back to The Old Grange.'

11

'We must keep track of the way back home,' Simon said. 'If we can direct the police back here before they realise we've escaped, there's a chance of capturing them.'

'Couldn't they be followed to wherever they've hidden the pictures, and the other things they stole?'

'Perhaps, but I'd rather get them in custody. Unless they've passed the things to another accomplice already, we'll find everything in the end.'

Linda nodded. She was tired and hungry. She hadn't eaten since breakfast, it was now after midnight, and various parts of her body ached or felt sore. She was also tingling with her memories of Simon's kisses. He'd been so suspicious, and then so tender, she was bewildered. Had it been affection, or was it that he'd felt remorse for his suspicions, and wanted to apologise? Or, and the thought gave her no satisfaction, had he merely been trying to comfort her for the dire situation they had been in?

The moon had risen, and outside the beam of the headlamps she could see ghostly shapes of trees and hedges. She tried to concentrate on the signposts they passed, frantically memorising them and the way Simon turned at junctions. He seemed to know the way, and half an hour after they left the clearing he turned into the gateway leading to the drive which wound through the farmland to the back of The Old Grange.

In the distance across the fields, she could see some tents remaining. The last of the re-enactors would be leaving tomorrow, Simon had told her. Many of them had too much to pack, or too far to go, to want to leave late on Sunday, when the spectators had finally departed.

Simon drove along a narrow track right into the courtyard, where lights still shone from the old dining room, and the modern kitchen. As he drew to a halt, Maggie appeared from one, the inspector and another policeman from the other. Simon gave a deep breath and stepped out of the car.

'Come on, we've still work to do, I'm afraid.'

Despite the inspector's weary demands that he be told at once all that had happened, Maggie insisted on supplying a huge pile of sandwiches.

'I made them earlier, and before you say a word I'm making a fresh pot of coffee. Would you like some as well?' she asked the inspector, and he nodded.

He ushered them into the dining room, and they almost fell into the nearest chairs.

'Before you start, we think they are hiding in a wood about twenty miles away,' Simon said. 'Have you a map?'

Silently Inspector Stone handed him one, and with occasional checking with Linda, Simon traced the way they had come.

'I think that's the track, but there are two, and I didn't notice if we passed another on the way to the main road. The car belongs to them, so you should find fingerprints.'

'Did you leave them there?'

'No, we escaped while they were gone, but they have a caravan and had left a light on, so we expect them to return. You might catch them during the night.'

'If they know you're gone, they'll move.'

Simon explained they'd covered their tracks and the inspector picked up the phone.

'I'll set things moving. Was there a second way out of the clearing?'

'A small path, not wide enough for a car. I think the way we came out is the only good track.'

At that moment, Maggie appeared with a loaded tray and poured out the coffee. When Linda stretched out for a sandwich Simon exclaimed and caught her hand, turning it up to look at the ends of her fingers.

'How did you rub them raw like this?'

'The nail, when I was twisting it,' she replied, trying to clench her hands into fists to hide them.

'You have some sort of fatal affinity with nails,' he said, raising her hand to his mouth and gently kissing the ends of her fingers. 'I'll deal with them as soon as you've eaten.'

Embarrassed, Linda glanced across at Maggie, and was surprised to find her smiling with what could only be described as maternal approval.

'Now, if you could explain,' Inspector Stone said with barely concealed impatience. 'Why did you leave the house when you'd been told to stay put, Miss Slater?'

Linda bridled at his tone.

'I knew Pete and no-one else did,' she insisted. 'OK, it was idiotic, Simon's already made that clear, but neither of us could have known he'd abduct us!'

'Tell me slowly, what happened after

you left the house?'

Linda complied, in between eating Maggie's delicious sandwiches and drinking the best-tasting coffee ever. The inspector listened, making notes, and asking questions occasionally. Then she and Simon described how Pete had captured them, and driven off before any alarm could be raised.

'When the horse came back to the stable, lathered and clearly frightened, we sent extra men to the exit gates, but we were too late. One of the stewards had seen a caravan and horse box leaving a few minutes earlier, but several caravans had gone during the earlier part of the afternoon, and we had no reason to suspect them in particular.'

'But weren't all the re-enactors staying for the rest of the display?' Linda asked.

'Some of the caravans belonged to spectators, who had been here on Saturday and probably wanted to get away before the rush. It was a bit odd to have the horse box leave, but the steward thought it had finished. He didn't know they were all taking part in the battles as well as the jousting, and for all he knew the horse leaving might have been lame or injured. He thought no more about it until we began to ask questions.'

Suddenly Linda yawned, and Simon stood up.

'Linda needs to go to bed. She's shattered. If we think of anything else we can tell you in the morning. You don't want me to come and show you the way to the clearing, do you?'

'No, Simon, you're exhausted, too, and your wrists need as much attention as my fingers!' Linda protested. 'The police can manage without you, surely.'

The inspector suppressed a smile.

'Do as the lady orders, Mr Cottrell,' he said. 'Go and anoint one another's wounds, and I'll speak to you both again in the morning, when perhaps I'll have been able to snatch a few hours' sleep myself.'

12

When Linda awoke, she lay in bed, recalling the kiss Simon had given her as he'd said good-night. Apart from the one cut on his forehead he was suffering from bruises, and her own roughened fingertips had not been serious. She was just contemplating whether to doze for longer or get up and have a shower when there was a tap on the door.

'Come in,' she called, expecting to see Maggie, and feeling guilty that while she had been lazing, the older woman had probably been up for hours, and was now bringing her tea.

The door opened to admit Simon, however, wearing a very smart business suit, and carrying a tray with a small teapot and two cups. Linda struggled up.

'How late is it? You shouldn't have

bothered, Simon.'

'After all the difficulty I had in persuading Maggie that it was perfectly respectable for me to enter a young lady's bedroom?' he said, affronted, setting down the tray on the bedside table and pouring out the tea. 'Milk and sugar? She has rather old-fashioned ideas, imagines I have never seen girls in rather fetching night-gowns.'

Linda chuckled, and looked down at the oversize T-shirt she wore in bed.

'I'm sure you've seen several,' she murmured, and felt a wave of disappointment engulf her when he merely grinned, handed her a cup, and didn't deny it.

Why should it matter to her? She liked him, he'd kissed her a couple of times, but they were strangers thrown together by odd circumstances, and she wasn't convinced he now believed her totally. Besides, she knew nothing about him. He might even be married, and such an attractive man had to have a girlfriend at least. He was speaking

115

again, and she dragged her wandering thoughts back to him.

'Maggie will give you breakfast and then Inspector Stone wants to see you. Eleanor's with him. Will you promise not to leave the house without her?'

'Where will you be? Are you going out?'

'I have an appointment in London, and have to leave in a few minutes. I'll be back for dinner this evening.'

He swallowed his own tea quickly, and with a brief wave departed. Linda sipped more slowly, then told herself not to be foolish. He hadn't said if Pete had been captured, but she was eager to know, and the sooner he was in custody the sooner she could return to her own flat. The thought depressed her, and she thrust away the implications as she showered and pulled on her jeans and shirt.

In the kitchen, Maggie, looking as fresh as though she had not sat up half the night waiting for them, was busy at the cooker.

'Full breakfast?' she asked, smiling. 'Coffee's made, and there are cereals on the dresser. Help yourself.'

'I don't think I could manage more than toast, thanks,' Linda said. 'It must be almost lunchtime.'

Maggie stared at her for a few moments, then turned away.

'White or brown bread?'

As Linda spread marmalade, Eleanor poked her head round the door, grinned and came in.

'Any coffee for me, Maggie?'

'Help yourself, girl.'

'What happened last night?' Linda asked.

'My fools of colleagues stamped their big feet all over the place, and somehow Pete and one of the others got away down another path and went to ground. At least we have one of them, but he's not talking yet.'

'Oh, no! Then Simon's still in danger if they catch up with him! And he's on his own today, gone to London!'

'Don't worry, he can look after

himself, and they won't know where he is. Besides, in a modern suit he doesn't look at all like a mediaeval knight, now does he?'

'He's still in danger,' Linda insisted, wishing she could rush after him, though judging by the past two days she wouldn't be much use — she'd been the cause of his being captured in the first place.

Eleanor reached over and squeezed her hand in sympathy.

'We have the car and the caravan and horse box, though, and plenty of evidence in there, plus your testimony, to put them away for a long time on abduction and false imprisonment charges, even if we can't pin the thefts here on them, and I'm sure we can do that. There were fingerprints on the door of the room where they left you, and they belong to a small-time hoodlum from London. Once we catch him he's got no defence.'

'What about Pete?'

'All his known haunts are being

watched. Inspector Stone wants to know all the places you went to, pubs and whatever, in case he has associates we might question. If you've finished eating, we can go across now.'

Linda did her best to recall everywhere she'd ever been with Pete, and the inspector relayed the information to the men who were trying to trace him. He was furious that Pete had slipped through their hands, and repeatedly warned Linda not to go anywhere on her own.

'He's bolder than we thought, and has cause to want revenge,' he said more than once.

'What about my brother and my parents?'

'Did Jackson know your family?'

'He knows where my parents live, but he never met them. He knows Bill, though.'

'Then we'll question your brother. He'll probably know other places where we can look.'

13

Linda spent the rest of the day fretting. When Simon returned at eight o'clock, she rushed out of the small sitting room where she and Eleanor had been watching television, and almost flung herself into his arms.

'Thank goodness, you're safe!' she exclaimed, and he swept her off her feet and swung her round until she was dizzy.

'You didn't think I could come to any harm in the big, bad metropolis, did you?' he teased, dropping a kiss on the end of her nose and putting her down. 'Has she been a good girl, Eleanor?'

'I'd hate to have her as a hospital patient,' Eleanor said. 'Every time we heard a car she had to go and see who it was, and she jumped a mile high whenever the phone rang. But she'll calm down now you're back. I bet you wish your students were as eager to see you!'

He grinned.

'Stay for dinner?' he asked Eleanor.

'No, thanks, I'd better go home. I'll be back in the morning, Linda. Have a good night.'

She winked at Simon and laughed, whisking out of the room as he threw a cushion after her.

Linda knew her cheeks were red at the innuendo, and was thankful when Simon excused himself to go and change.

'I'm stifled in this suit,' he said, tearing off his tie. 'I won't be more than five minutes.'

Maggie had laid the table in the small breakfast room near the kitchen, and despite the light evening she had drawn the curtains and lit candles. A single red rose was in a slender crystal vase, and two wine glasses were by each place.

When Simon came back and ushered her into the room Linda could not suppress a gasp of admiration.

'Does the aristocracy live like this all the time?' she asked as they were sampling fresh melon balls, before reflecting that this was a rather gauche question.

Simon, however, laughed, and poured her some wine.

'Try this. It's another of our ventures, a vineyard, and we're not aristocracy. My great-great-great grandfather was given a title, just a baronetcy, in the nineteenth century, because he made a lot of money out of shipping. His son became a merchant banker and made another fortune. We've been lucky to be able to stay here, had some good investments, and the property passed on to the heir in time to minimise death duties. Besides, it's only a modest little manor house by stately home standards, and the farm and stud help to keep it viable. When Rupert, my eldest brother, inherits, I imagine I'll take over the stud full time.'

'Won't you be sorry to leave teaching?'

'No. I always knew that was just a

temporary career.'

He paused, and Maggie came in to clear the dishes.

'Sorry, Simon, but the inspector's on the phone, and he says it can't wait,' she said.

'Let's hope they've caught him.'

He went out, and it was several minutes before he reappeared, holding the door open for Maggie who carried on a tray a casserole and vegetable dishes.

'A ragout, with new potatoes and fresh peas,' she said, lifting the lid, beaming proudly.

Linda sniffed appreciatively.

'That smells delicious. The vegetables are home-grown?'

'Yes, we grow most of our own. That way I know they're always fresh,' Maggie replied.

She departed, and Simon chuckled.

'Maggie has a fetish about fresh vegetables, and fresh everything else. Mother bought her a huge freezer years ago, thinking she would store the surplus, but I don't think she ever uses it apart from making ice cubes. What she doesn't want is sold in the farm shop.'

'Have they caught Pete? Was that what Inspector Stone rang for?' Linda demanded.

'Not yet. He wanted to come and speak to you later, so I said nine o'clock.'

Linda fretted, but Simon refused to talk about Pete, saying he was bored with hearing all about Linda's boyfriend.

She then worried that he seemed to have reverted to disbelieving her innocence.

She tried to refuse the strawberries and cream Maggie brought in, as the clock was striking nine, but Maggie looked so disappointed, saying the pesky inspector could wait, that Linda laughed and took them.

'I've shown Inspector Stone into the small sitting room,' Maggie said, 'and I'll serve coffee there, for all of you.'

Linda almost ran along the corridor, but Simon clasped her arm and forced her to slow down.

'Steady, calm down,' he said, and she bit her lip and tried to take deep breaths.

'I just want to know he's behind bars and I can get back to normal,' she explained.

She didn't, she knew, for getting back to normal would be the end of her time with Simon.

Against that she did want to feel safe once more, so that both of them could move around without fearing some sudden attack. She greeted the inspector with a strained, questioning smile, but he did no more than nod a greeting, and waited while Maggie served coffee.

★   ★   ★

When they all had coffee, and Simon and the inspector had brandies, he turned to her.

'Miss Slater, we're no further forward, I'm afraid. Your brother gave us a few more leads, and your cousin did, too, after we had applied a little pressure, but they've led nowhere. So I came to ask if you would help once more.'

'What more can I do?' she asked, puzzled. 'I've told you all I can possibly remember about Pete, all the people I know who might have known him.'

'And we've questioned all of them, and his workmates, and even several of his customers. None of them knows much about him, in fact most of them knew less than you'd already told us.'

'So how can I help?'

Simon had been standing leaning against the fireplace.

He put his cup and glass down with great deliberation and stepped forward so that he was looking over the inspector, seated in a low, comfortable armchair.

'No, I don't think you can ask Linda to do this, inspector,' he said evenly.

'It's for her to decide.'

'And she'll do it because we have, between us, made her feel guilty about the theft, and the abduction, and she'll want to make amends, but it's too risky. You don't know what Jackson might do, and you can't guard against every possible eventuality.'

'I wish you'd both stop discussing me as though I were not here,' Linda exclaimed, annoyed. 'What will I agree to do? And what danger is there? You might at least give me the opportunity to hear what it is, and choose for myself!'

Simon glanced at her, then shrugged.

'Of course, you'll be told, but remember there is absolutely no need for you to agree,' he said. 'The inspector is impatient to solve the case, but we were the people harmed. It was my family property that was stolen, and we were the ones abducted. We have a right to say whether we agree to what he proposes or not, Linda. Remember that, please.'

'Miss Slater must decide, Mr Cottrell. You have no right to influence her,' Inspector Stone said coldly.

Simon opened his mouth and then snapped it shut. He turned away and picked up his brandy goblet, drained the fiery liquid in one gulp, and sat down on the settee next to Linda.

'Go ahead.'

Inspector Stone inclined his head gravely.

'Miss Slater, when we tried to capture Jackson last night he was swearing that if it hadn't been for you he'd have got away with the stolen goods, and that whatever happened he would get his own back on you.'

Linda shivered, and found Simon's hand closed over hers. She clutched at it convulsively.

'I would have expected him to make threats, but what is it you want me to do?'

'We think he's in hiding, with people we know nothing about. We don't know where the third man is yet, and if he lives nearby, Jackson may have a bolthole with him. But he will be aware of what's going on, we're sure of that.'

'How?'

'He could be watching police activity. We don't know what criminal acquaintances he has, who could be telling him what is happening. We want to flush him out.'

Simon could keep quiet no longer. Linda had felt his hand tightening as they listened to the inspector's measured words, and she turned to look at him as he leaned forward.

'And they want to bait the trap with you!' he said. 'They'll set the trap, leave you helpless, and then make the same sort of mess trying to catch him as they have done so far!'

'Mr Cottrell, that's not fair. None of us has behaved with complete success, have we?'

Simon subsided but did not let go his grip on Linda's hand.

'No, and I apologise. Linda must decide, but I hope she says no,' he said worriedly.

'If you'd stop arguing and tell me what you want me to do, I might just be able to do that!'

'We want you to go back to your flat tomorrow, Miss Slater, openly, and letting some of your workmates know. Perhaps you could telephone them and inform them you'll be returning to work on Wednesday, and drop hints of something exciting you have to tell them.

'What we hope is that somehow Jackson will hear about this, or he may even be able to overlook your flat, or have an accomplice who can. We're sure we have actually stumbled across the fringes of a bigger organisation than we thought at first.'

'And then what? Pete knows I'm back home and comes to attack me again? Is that what you want me to do?'

'Don't do it, Linda. Don't agree!' Simon exclaimed.

'We'll have men concealed, ready to protect you, ready to capture him as soon as he shows his face. Well, Miss Slater, will you help us?'

14

Simon leaned across from his driver's seat in the car and kissed Linda, but his worried face was grim and the kiss he gave her was no more than a peck on the cheek.

'For the benefit of any watchers,' he said, his voice curt. 'I think you're mad to agree to this.'

'If it's the only way to catch him,' Linda said wearily, 'I'd rather try it.'

They'd argued until midnight, long after Inspector Stone had gone, and he'd tried to persuade her to change her mind. He'd tried again that morning, and now, at almost noon, he hadn't given up his attempts to get her to back down as they arrived at her flat.

'The police have men installed in several of the houses round about,' she said now.

'They can't put someone in a car or

van, watching, which would be the best way of keeping surveillance. It's too obvious. Jackson would spot that straight away.'

'No, but they'll have different vehicles patrolling all the time, and I have this alarm which will alert them without him knowing,' she said, fingering the pendant which was disguised to look like a locket. 'You'd better go, Simon. He might be watching.'

She stepped from the car, took her case from the back seat, walked a little way down the path, turned and waved. Simon let in the clutch and drove off down the road.

Linda had never felt so alone in all her life. She went down the stairs and opened her front door.

Inspector Stone had told her they'd installed various devices in the flat, and they were utterly certain no-one was lying in wait, but she still had to summon up all her resolution not to turn and flee, but to open the door and step inside.

There was a small pile of letters on the mat, and she automatically stooped to pick them up. Most were circulars, which she threw into the waste bin, or bills which she set aside to deal with later, when all this was over.

She couldn't concentrate now. There were two personal letters. She recognised the handwriting on one envelope as that of an old schoolfriend who now lived in London, and put that aside, too. She wasn't in the mood for Vicky's gossip.

The final envelope had been hand-delivered, and her heart began to hammer as she slit it open.

There was one sheet of paper, and the message, though longer, was as uncompromising as the previous one she had received.

You didn't obey me before, and now it's too late. When I've dealt with your mother I'll be back for you, however long I have to wait for you to come home.

Her immediate instinct was to rush

out and go to make sure her mother was safe, but this could well be playing into Pete's hands. Linda shivered, and reached for her mobile phone.

She had to report this. The police would give her mother protection. The man who eventually answered the contact number she'd been given was calmly brisk.

'Don't worry, lass, your parents are being watched, so's your brother. That monster can't get to them, and he'd be running too many risks. It's you he wants.'

This was hardly reassuring, Linda reflected as she switched off. She unpacked her case, hung up her clothes or put them to be washed. Then she went through into her tiny kitchen and began to prepare a snack.

Act normally, they'd said, but she had no desire to eat. She'd forced down some dry toast that morning, but it had taken great self-control even to nibble half a slice.

Pete might wait until darkness, which

in the middle of June was as late as it could be. Linda breathed deeply to calm herself. She wanted it to be over as quickly as possible, and she had to stay in control. She could not afford to relax her guard for one minute.

She made a sandwich and tried to eat, but couldn't. Instead of coffee, she mixed a sachet of instant soup, and smiled faintly as she wondered what Maggie would say.

She sipped it slowly, and longed for a shower, but to undress was to make herself too vulnerable.

Then the telephone shrilled, and she spilled the remains of the soup down her shirt as she jumped convulsively. For a moment she stared at it. The answerphone was blinking at her, but she hadn't thought to check her messages.

She'd better answer. She was supposed to be telephoning friends in any case, and this might be one of them.

Gingerly she picked up the receiver and almost collapsed with relief when she heard Jane, her boss, ask how she was.

'Has the sickness bug been defeated?' Jane asked.

Recalling the excuse Simon had phoned in to her office on Monday morning, Linda muttered a reply.

He'd done it without consulting her because, he said, she'd been fast asleep. Linda frowned at the reminder of his presumption, and then longed for him to be there with her.

'I'll be in tomorrow,' she managed to say.

'Are you sure? You sound odd,' Jane said. 'Take another day or two if you don't feel up to it. Business is slow at the moment. We can cope without you.'

'I'll see how I feel. Thanks,' Linda replied.

Jane soon broke the connection, and Linda listened to her messages. One was from a friend, miffed because she hadn't been at the local pub, as they'd agreed, for a drink on Sunday morning. She'd have to ring her. One was from her mother asking where Bill was, because he hadn't turned up for lunch on Sunday.

'But then, why I should ever depend on him I don't know,' her mother added.

Why hadn't he gone? Linda began to worry. Her brother was not one to refuse a free meal, and her mother's Sunday lunches were legendary. But the police had reassured her he was being watched, protected. He must be all right.

Then there were several calls where the callers had hung up without leaving a message. Were they from Pete? She wished she had one of those machines that recorded details such as the times of calls, and numbers, but that didn't help now.

The final call was from another friend, and she'd given the date and time, nine o'clock on Monday morning.

So the other calls, if they had been from Pete, could have been coming in during the night, after she and Simon had escaped from the horse box, after Pete had escaped from the police trap.

There were no more, but that proved nothing. If he was indeed watching the flat, or had someone doing this for him, as the police suspected, they'd know she wasn't there. Restlessly she prowled round the flat. It was a glorious, summer day, and normally, home during the afternoon, she'd have been outside in her small patch of garden, weeding the flower beds or just enjoying the sun.

But she dared not open the doors and go outside. She was the bait in the trap, and the police wanted to catch Pete as he approached. Outside she would be too exposed.

The afternoon wore on. Linda was too tense to concentrate on anything, too afraid of giving way to seek the consolation of human voices over the telephone. She switched on the TV, but decided it might mask noises, and she needed to be able to hear all that went on, be prepared for Pete if he came.

Then, nervous of the silence, she put on some music and turned it as low as it would go.

Every few minutes she wandered into the bedroom and peered out of the window from behind the curtains. There was nothing to see, just the occasional pedestrian's head visible from her semi-basement, or a car or van passing by.

Which of these, she wondered, contained her police guards.

She decided to change her shirt, splashed by the soup. She'd meant to do it straight away, and then listening to the messages on her answerphone had distracted her, and she'd forgotten. She pulled it over her head, and at that precise moment the front door bell rang.

Frantic, terrified, Linda seized the clean T-shirt she'd pulled out of the drawer and struggled into it.

'I'm coming,' she called as the bell pealed once more, but before she reached the hallway she froze.

The door was opening, and footsteps sounded on the tiles.

'You can't hide, Linda. I know you're there.'

Pete slammed the door behind him, and Linda shrank back into the bedroom.

Why hadn't the police caught him before he got in? Wide-eyed, she watched as he came towards her. He had one hand in his pocket, and she was sure it concealed a gun.

'Why did you betray me, Linda?' he asked in a cool, calm voice. 'We could have been so good together, you know. I'd have looked after you. I'd have given you anything you wanted. The silver alone in that collection would keep us in luxury for a year, and the paintings would have fetched much more. And I have other stuff, gathered before I met you. I've been preparing for years.'

'Where are they?' Linda asked.

If she could keep him talking for long enough there was a chance the police would come. Pete smiled, an unpleasant grimace.

'Oh, you don't trick me like that.'

'Why did you ever think I'd agree to it?'

'Your cousin said you would, and Bill didn't seem averse to a spot of quick profit. It was your misfortune you had foolish scruples about robbing your new boyfriend.'

'Simon's not — ' she began, but Pete laughed again.

'Had you met him before Saturday? You were certainly very close very quickly. I didn't know you were such a quick worker, Linda. You didn't encourage me so fast, but then, he already has the money, doesn't he? He doesn't have to work for it like us poor devils.'

'If you call theft and abducting people work, you're mad!' Linda exclaimed, anger at his words overcoming her fear.

'Never mind the insults. You're coming with me now, and we'll see how much lover-boy is prepared to pay to get you free.'

Where were the police?

Linda prayed they would be waiting outside, but then she realised that was unlikely. Pete might be doing all sorts of things to her inside the flat, even killing her, and they'd promised to protect her. Perhaps it would be safer to get outside as soon as possible, and pray they would be there, or at least someone would be there who might help her.

She moved towards the door, but Pete thrust her back and she fell on to the bed.

'Oh, no. We have unfinished business, and it will be finished right here,' he said wickedly.

Slowly he drew his hand out of his pocket, and Linda blinked, biting back the scream in her throat. In his hand he held a small revolver. Mesmerised, she stared at it.

Where were the police?

As Pete raised his hand, there was a noise from the living room, and he swung round, pointing the gun towards the door. Then all hell seemed to break loose.

Linda heard the front door being kicked in, followed by a shot which shattered her dressing-table mirror, and more breaking glass as the window to the side of her was kicked in and a body hurtled through.

'On the floor, quick!'

She almost sobbed with relief. It was Simon, and he grabbed her arm and bundled her unceremoniously on to the floor where they were shielded by the bed. Pete was shooting wildly, first into the sitting room, then towards the front door, and once a bullet pinged into the skirting board just by her head.

After a minute there was silence, and then Pete began to curse. Simon raised his head cautiously, and then rose to his feet. Linda wanted to pull him back, but she guessed all the bullets in the revolver had been used, and there was a chance to overpower Pete before he could reload.

She peered over the side of the bed to see Pete frantically dragging something out of his pocket, but before he could reload Simon had launched himself round the end of the bed, rugby-tackling Pete and bringing him crashing to the floor.

Pete howled with rage, and wriggled furiously, while Simon struggled to hang on to him.

What had happened to the police, Linda wondered.

Then, afraid Pete was getting free of Simon's hold, she looked round for a weapon. The only remotely heavy thing was her old hair dryer. She yanked it from the socket and scrambled across the bed, bringing it down with a satisfying clunk on to Pete's head.

He grunted with pain, and Simon held the revolver tight against Pete's body. Linda hit Pete again, and then, to her immense relief, a large policeman scrambled through the shattered window, brandishing a pair of handcuffs.

15

One of the policemen, the one who had entered through the garden and sitting room, had been shot in the leg, but was comfortable in hospital. The one who had come in by the front door had retreated in the face of gunfire, and followed Simon through the window instead. Three more piled in within seconds and whisked their wounded colleague and Pete away. Inspector Stone remained.

Linda was contemplating her many broken windows rather ruefully, and then she turned to Simon and began to laugh.

'You look a fright,' she said. 'But thanks for coming at just the right moment, and looking so impressive!'

Simon was looking at his long, grey balding wig, which had suffered badly during the brief tussle with Pete. He still had the make-up on his face, giving him dozens of wrinkles, and bits of his straggling grey beard had come unstuck and were clinging to the disreputable old sweater, filthy and full of holes, that he still wore. He had on baggy trousers, tied below the knee with string, and incongruously, new but dirty trainers.

'I need a good scrub,' he said.

The inspector glared at him.

'You disobeyed orders to keep away.'

'It was perhaps as well,' Simon replied coolly. 'If you thought I was going to leave Linda here, unprotected, you had another think coming. I'm able to disguise myself as a mediaeval knight, and it was no problem to act like a sozzled, old man sleeping off the drink on a convenient piece of grass. Where were your chaps when Jackson barged his way in?'

'They were on their way, but they had to approach with caution so as not to alarm him,' Inspector Stone said, rather defensively. 'However, in the end you did no harm, so we'll forget about it.'

'I should think you will! Did you get the other one, the fellow who was skulking around outside?'

'Yes. We're not as incompetent as you think, Mr Cottrell, and for your information he's singing loudly. We'll most probably have your stolen goods in our possession by this evening. Now, Miss Slater, you can't stay here. I've ordered the windows to be boarded up if a glazier can't be found to replace the glass today, but you ought not to be alone. Can you go and stay with your parents for the time being?'

'She'll stay with me,' Simon announced. 'Have you contacted her brother?'

'Yes. He'd gone to stay with a friend when he received threats from Jackson. We've interviewed him, but he knew even less than you, Miss Slater. He'd apparently met Jackson in a pub only the day before he introduced him to you. So I can contact you at The Old Grange?'

'Yes, for the foreseeable future,' Simon replied.

Linda's heart gave a jump. Apart from not wanting to have to answer their questions and listen to her parents' endless demands to tell them how all this had happened, she was glad Simon was not abandoning her. She would have at least a few more days with him. They might have time to talk of normal things, and she would find out more about him, such as whether he had a serious girlfriend, she thought.

'I'll come and report to you later tonight then. Where's your car?' the inspector asked.

'In the multi-storey carpark in the middle of town. Linda can pack a bag and if she doesn't mind accompanying an old layabout I'll carry it for her.'

'We'll spare her that. I can give you a lift.'

A couple of hours later, clean and relaxed after a soak in the bath, Linda was wondering what to wear for dinner. She'd packed in a hurry, mainly jeans and shirts, but she had thought to include a couple of skirts and the lacy blouse she'd worn before. She decided the blue skirt would be best, and was just spraying on perfume when Simon knocked at her door and entered.

He was wearing black trousers and a red silk shirt, and restored to his normal handsome self. Her heart, which seemed to be behaving very erratically today, gave a sudden flip.

'That feels better,' he said. 'I had to smell the part as well as look it, and it's amazingly difficult to acquire a really disgusting niff in a hurry.'

'Yes, I was rather glad you had an open-topped car to drive home in,' Linda said, smiling. 'How did you obtain the pong? It doesn't come in bottles, like perfume.'

'Apart from telling you I visited the stables and the town rubbish dump on my way back to you, you don't want to know. Those things will all be burned and thank goodness the covers on my car seats are detachable and can be cleaned.'

Linda stood up.

'I was so very glad to see you, pong and all,' she said shyly. 'I really thought the police had messed it all up and he was going to shoot me.'

Simon's eyes darkened.

'I wouldn't have let him. Are you ready? Maggie said dinner was prompt at eight, and I never keep Maggie waiting. But I want time for a drink first.'

He took her hand and led her down the stairs, but not into the breakfast room as on the previous night.

'Maggie thought that as this was a celebration, we should use the formal dining room,' he said, 'so we'll have a drink in the library next door. The drawing room is too empty and it's too big a reminder of what we might have lost.'

'Have the police found your things then?'

'Yes. They rang to say that as far as they could see everything was still in the horse box. They hadn't even unpacked it. I have to go and identify it in the morning.'

She hadn't been in the library before. It hadn't been open to visitors touring the house. It was a large room, two big tables with chairs around them, computers on each, bookshelves on every available wall, and a group of shabby, leather chairs grouped round the fireplace.

By one chair was a wine cooler, and a bottle of champagne waited, glasses beside it. Simon indicated she sit, and he opened the champagne, poured two glasses, and came to hand her one then sit in the chair opposite.

'Here's to a successful conclusion.'

Linda drank, and didn't know what else to say. She looked round the room for inspiration.

'Is this where you began to be interested in history?' she asked. 'Was your father a historian?'

'Not in the professional sense, though he researched the family history back to the sixteenth century. But for the next year I'll be working here a good deal. I'm not sure if I'll be living at the Grange, though. I might get myself a house in the village, or even in the town.'

'Why? I thought your college was somewhere in the West country.'

'It is, but I'm taking a year off, a sabbatical. The man I went to see in London was a publisher. He's interested in a book I mean to write, about the crusades. Of course, I shall have to do quite a bit of travelling, following the routes the crusaders took, visiting all their castles, as well as sitting here writing it.'

'That will be interesting,' Linda said.

Her hopes that she and Simon might see more of one another once her flat was in a fit state for her to return to took a dive. He'd be close at hand, not in his distant college, but only for some of the time.

'It would be more interesting if I had company,' he said, and rose to come across and take her glass from her.

Carefully he set both glasses down on the table, and then sat on the arm of her chair.

'Did Pete mean much to you?' he asked. 'Was it serious, before you discovered he was a crook?'

She shook her head.

'I liked him, he was good company, and once or twice I thought it might become more serious, but I'm not heart-broken, if that's what you're asking.'

'Good. Linda, I don't want to rush things. You've had a very stressful few days, and lots of shocks, but when I kissed you, something happened to me. I meant it just for comfort, but it turned into a raging need for you, and frightened me. I'd never felt that before. I want to get to know you better, spend as much time with you as I can, and if in time you can feel the same about me, maybe we can have a future together. I'm not asking for an answer. I know it's much too soon, but will you humour me?'

Linda was bemused. He couldn't be saying this. She shook her head to clear away the mists, and Simon sighed, and rose to his feet.

'I'm sorry, I knew it was too soon to speak. Forget I said anything. But I hope you won't hold it against me, and we might be friends.'

'Stop it!' Linda commanded.

'I'm sorry,' he began, but she jumped to her feet and grasped his hands.

'Simon, stop talking and let me get a word in edgeways! I don't need time, I don't want to humour you. It was the same for me, when you kissed me, I mean. I wanted it to go on and on, but I never thought I had a chance. You thought I was such an idiot, and I imagined you were only helping me out of kindness, and perhaps to get your pictures and things back.'

He was holding her by the shoulders, looking intently into her eyes.

'You mean it? Linda, can you

possibly mean you love me, like I do you?'

Wordlessly she nodded, and he folded her into his arms. She lifted up her face and felt she would drown in the bliss of his embrace. It felt like coming home. She knew she would never again be alone, or frightened.

Some time later, there was a discreet cough, and they broke apart, glancing towards the door.

'I said eight sharp for dinner, Simon, but I understand you have more important things on your mind,' Maggie said, beaming fondly at them.

Simon laughed.

'Sorry, Maggie, but I think, though I haven't actually asked her yet, you can congratulate me. We'll come right away.'

'Good, it's about time you found a good woman and settled down, and Miss Linda's the right one for you. I knew that straight away. I'm glad I cooked a special dinner, and bring that champagne with you.'

'She's a tyrant,' Simon grumbled as

he reluctantly let Linda go and picked up the drinks' cooler.

'Do you really mean you'll marry me?' he asked some time later, when, after a superb meal, they were settled in the library again, curled up together on one of the big, comfortable chairs.

'How many times do you need telling?' she asked, twining her fingers round his. 'I fell in love with you when I saw you jousting. There's something so romantic about a full suit of armour, though it's not very comfortable. Oh, Simon, I didn't dare dream of it! And if it hadn't been for Pete we'd never have met.'

'One thing's certain, we'll not invite him to the wedding. Now, when's the soonest we can get married? Next week? My parents will be back late tomorrow, and in the morning we'll go and buy a ring, two rings, engagement and wedding rings, and start looking for a house. Where would you prefer to be?'

'Simon, stop!' Linda said, laughing. 'I

need a little longer than a week to plan everything.'

He laughed, and began to kiss her again, and Linda forgot the practical arrangements as she revelled in the feeling of security and excitement he gave her.

THE END

We do hope that you have enjoyed reading this large print book.

Did you know that all of our titles are available for purchase?

We publish a wide range of high quality large print books including:
Romances, Mysteries, Classics
General Fiction
Non Fiction and Westerns

Special interest titles available in large print are:
The Little Oxford Dictionary
Music Book, Song Book
Hymn Book, Service Book

Also available from us courtesy of Oxford University Press:
Young Readers' Dictionary
(large print edition)
Young Readers' Thesaurus
(large print edition)

For further information or a free brochure, please contact us at:
Ulverscroft Large Print Books Ltd.,
The Green, Bradgate Road, Anstey,
Leicester, LE7 7FU, England.
Tel: (00 44) **0116 236 4325**
Fax: (00 44) **0116 234 0205**

PERILOUS JOURNEY

Caroline Joyce

After the execution of Charles I,
Louisa's Royalist father considers it
too dangerous for her to stay in
England and arranges for her to go
to the Isle of Man with Armand de
la Tremouille, the nephew of the
island's Royalist Governor. Their
ship is boarded by Parliamentarians
who plan to sail for Ireland, but a
storm causes them to be ship-
wrecked on the Calf of Man.
Magnus Stapleton, the Parliamen-
tarian chief, becomes infatuated
with Louisa, but she has fallen in
love with Armand.

THE GYPSY'S RETURN

Sara Judge

After the death of her cruel father, Amy Keene's step-brother and step-sister treated her just as badly. Amy had two friends, old Dr. Hilland and the washerwoman, Rosalind, with her fatherless child Becky. When Rosalind falls ill, Amy is entrusted with a letter to be given to Becky on her marriage. When the letter's contents are discovered, it causes Amy both mental and physical suffering and sets the seal of fate upon Rosalind's gypsy friend, Elias Jones.

WEB OF DECEIT

Margaret McDonagh

A good-looking man turned up on Louise's doorstep one day, introducing himself as Daniel Kinsella, an Australian friend of her brother-in-law, Greg. He said he had come to stay whilst he did some research — apparently Greg had written to her about it. Louise's initial reaction was to turn him away, but he was very persuasive. However, she was to discover that Daniel had bluffed his way into her life, and soon she found herself caught up in his dangerous mission.